Fate

Tragedy

Fate
Tragedy

RODERICK HOWARD

FATE TRAGEDY

iUniverse books may be ordered through booksellers or by contacting:

iUniverse
1663 Liberty Drive
Bloomington, IN 47403
www.iuniverse.com
844-349-9409

Because of the dynamic nature of the Internet, any web addresses or links contained in this book may have changed since publication and may no longer be valid. The views expressed in this work are solely those of the author and do not necessarily reflect the views of the publisher, and the publisher hereby disclaims any responsibility for them.

Any people depicted in stock imagery provided by Getty Images are models, and such images are being used for illustrative purposes only. Certain stock imagery © Getty Images.

ISBN: 978-1-6632-1826-1 (sc)
ISBN: 978-1-6632-1827-8 (e)

Print information available on the last page.

iUniverse rev. date: 02/12/2021

Dedications:

This book is dedicated to my cousin Chanel Wodbury

(R.I.P) and my late Grandmother Doralee Howard

(R.I.P.). Let their souls stay in the hands of God

Introduction

The pearly white gates are in your head as you take your exit photo to leave prison. You take urine as well, all in one day. Maxed out. No programs or no parole. Nobody you have to answer to and no more fines having to pay once a month. Everyday would be something different. You are seeing different people inside of the facility doing all paperwork that involves you leaving prison. Making sure you have bus tickets to make it all the way home without having to ask for help. Getting your inmate account together so you can receive a prepaid card with the remainder of your money to go with you. At this time you are sitting with a group of people either going home the same day as you or going to a program upon being released. The day is a good day knowing your time is coming again.

You can't wait to leave. You are having a hard time sleeping at night. You are going to your sisters house in which your mom had to convience her to allow you to stay there. After all the things you did and do for your sister because she is your sister, you are feeling some type of way but you don't let it break you swag. Its cool but not. As log as you get out it will be cool. You will make a way. The days wine down and the nights seem longer but nature is going to move the way it suppose to. You workout even harder. Keeping track of your weight goal which is 200lbs. You are just at that if not more. You are already bigger than you ever been.

You exchange information with the people you plan on keeping in touch with. You kick it with your cousin who goal is to be a big rapper. He is on his way. He just had to get the time out the way so when he blow up bigger, he don't have to worry about bullshit programs neither. He have a gift for it. A label is already waiting for him to come home. You both are going to make it. With him and your brother achieving their goals give you the motivation to achieve more as well. On the way to the top as he would say. You have to get the engine rolling as well.

Figuring out what you will do for work and what's going on out there in the streets. You just know you will not be selling drugs anymore. Getting rich or die trying as 50 cent would say is the motto.

The day come before you are maxing out. You give all your food away. Splitting it with your cousin, in which he already had food and your roommate. You had to pack up that night because when the morning come your stuff is already ready to go and you are off the count. Protocol. You can't go to sleep because knowing the next day is your release date. Talking about being exciting. Finally

The night came and went and your name is called early. Right after breakfast you had to grab your things and head to admissions. Nervous because you have been locked up for months and you don't know how to control yourself. The procejure is for you to grab your ID, state your name and number, change into your clothes that they give everyone to leave in, then wait until transportation gets there to take all who is leaving to the train station. You can catch the train or the bus, your choice. As everyone is waiting your name is called because your mom is outside waiting for you. She on the other side of the gates make you even more happy to leave the belly of the beast. Here goes your fate....

Chapter 1

FATE: What has been spoken; the cause or will or will that is held to determine events.

It felt good having you name called to hit the front gates to leave that black whole where the justice system put guys who in there eyes commit crimes. A cold pit stop. The gates open up finally a free man and your mother is waiting for her son with open arms. Her son is back home with ambition to be successful. Hugging her with a big smile it for sure felt like freedom. Your mother was happy to see you in 28 and a half months. She was wearing clothes that was dressed to impress. Your sister was sitting in the car with your mother. At the moment you were thinking you were going out to eat. There was another thing in stored that was not said to you for a reason. You sat in the car ready for the world, but news came to you like a big bag of bricks. Your sister noticed that what the news was you have not been told. Out of curiousity you had to ask a question. You mother answered the question by stating that your grandmother had passed away and the funeral is about to start. Talk about a stormy day. The day was suppose to be a happy day because of your release instead you were going straight to a funeral. Bummer.

You begin to cry to the fact that you were expecting to come home and see your grandmother alive not dead. Your grandmother was your heart and she had a heart of gold. The words can not express how much you loved your grandmother. You thought of her throughout your state bid and now she is gone and will never be forgotten. You would wash her clothes whenever she needed to by walking a few blocks with a big bag of dirty laundry to your house to get washed then walk them back down to her. You got everything she wanted that was in your power to do. Everything from a pack of cigarettes to a can of beer. Anything and everything was hers.

The pain runs deep as you ride down the highway to hell to a damn funeral. Nice day huh? The family only time your dad side of the family comes together is when a tragedy happens. You love seeing them all and you knew the family would love to see you to because you have been away and you have your weight all the way up.

Your grandmother wanted to have all of the family together anyway and she got what she wanted its just crazy how it had to happen this way.

You arrive at the church fresh out of prison for all to see. You still felt bad but an event like a funeral makes you stronger. Tears of joy or pain. Sorrow and guilt. Testemonies come from the family and all remind those listening ears how your grandmother invited any and everybody inside her home. Regardless of she knows you or not you were welcomed. Her home was your home. As the funeral comes to an end the last time to see her before her casket closes and back to the earth she came.

We all go to the grave site. The flowers are placed on the casket. Then after she is given a farewell everybody meet at a hall to eat and remember a queen as risen. You had a couple of dollars and you hooked up with your female cousin and went to the liquor store to buy some apple Amsterdam and a pack of cigarettes. You are celebrating the freedom of the both of two people you and your grandmother.

Still a beautiful day but and never forgotten. You hid the Amsterdam in your cousins purse. Your uncle catches you and wanted in as well. Now all three of you guys are taking shots to glorify freedom. The bottle is gone and the eaten up. Everybody decided to go their separate ways but you three came up with plan to continue the party elsewhere. Your mother takes your belongings. The next step is to figure out who was buying the next bottle. You guy decided to go to your uncles how to keep the drinking going. You drink slow because you just came home from prison.

Your mind is furious and you wanted to show the world that you as a convicted felon you can change. Day one is said but beautiful. Your cousin said her house to sleep. Her boyfriend is at work and we can chill and catch up on the times that were lost. She mention that it was a female from your past that was at the funeral that wanted to see you and you were fresh fish for the females and she thought she was the first to get some of you. She lived just a few doors away and she wanted she wanted to end the night with your company.

You arrived at your cousin house but she was arguing with her man that was suppose to be at work. You was not going to let him disrespect her but you did not get in the middle of the argument. He walks out and she was drunk and falls to sleep but before she goes to sleep you make sure your cousin is okay. You locked the door and walks to the friends house. You arrive at your old friends house with the rest of the bottle and she was tipsy too. You said to yourself that you were going to lay it on her.

Her son was woke and they started to have a discussion about his goals were. You tried to stay out of it but he asked your opinion. You was not beat about the subject and answered it with a short statement. As a parent and a person from the outside looking in you gave your opinion. The mother wanted him to play sports. She wanted him to get a scholarship to do so and he disagreed because to him it was more recreational thing to him and he wanted to do something else that was more interesting to him. He wanted to do something that was bigger and a better move for himself. I agreed because sometimes the parents feel is right for the child, but it may not be interesting to the child. She told you to shut up and mind your business in a very aggressive manner because it was her house. You took into consideration that it was her house and you did not want to intrude.

Her and son again asked you your opinion again. You hesitate to answer but because he was actually right. At the moment the raft came upon you. His mother said if you were not going to sleep on the couch or you will be getting kicked out. You took door number 2 and left the house. You walk to the bus stop and just so happen to have a bus ticket on you. She tried to tell you it was cold outside and to come inside but you declined and jumped on the bus. A nice bus ride soothes the mind. Your brother in law was up late playing Call of duty and he just happen to be up. Good shit. She was up she would be getting on your ass. You expressed how you felt and you was not going to actually going to be their long. Who mad now. Your mother practicely begged your sister to allow you to stay there. She had a good reason because you do be wilding at times. You do own up to your past actions, but if a person hold your past against you, they mine as well be the prosecutor themselves. Burn him.

As you play the city a little, you see who is still on the streets. Dead or alive or locked up the city is different you can not walk without the police all in your face because you are a new face to them. Knowing you may have warrants you still walk with pride and confidence. You are use to it knowing you have a lot of confidence in yourself.

Where you are at in your sister house you are in the back room downstairs there is a curtain that seperete the back room and the kitchens. You in to your ways and that's smoking and drinking. You look for your brother but you can't find him. You just happen to be downtown and bump onto him getting off the bus. Just getting out of work he tells you he lives in the area of your sister. He is your motivation to continue to achieve your goals. While speaking to him he talks about that he is also attempting to reach his goals. His skills are miraculous and he can out rap the next big thing and anybody who is already in the industry. You both walk home instead of catching the bus. While on your walk he gives you a couple of dollars, doing what a real brother does. His rap name is Superstar Ace.

You both explain how things are going and the roads both are taking to get there. He asked you if you needed a job and if so he could get you in the place he was. Another blessing you would get for being around him. Both you to positive auras would rub off on each other. Napolean Hill once stated, "You must surround yourself with people that are striving for the same thing as you are. If success is what they want in life then be around that person because you want the same thing". " Laws of Success", is one of the many books you enjoyed reading by the author.

You push Ace to be even more successful even though he already is going hard at his ambition but his ambition is also a push for you. Once everything is a go you both will enjoy the fruits of the labor put in and look back at where you both came from and how much work you both had to put in to get there. Blood brothers until the grave.

You get a job as a busser at P.F. Chang's in Malton where Ace work at. He got you in there. It is a Chinese resturant. It is a classy resturant with a different crowd. Lights are dim at night and slow music play across the speaker. They have the usual eating tables and a bar where a person can sit and enjoy their drinks watching the sports games that come on tv. Either it be football, hockey, baseball, soccer, or any other sport that comes on tv the place had it on. A nice atmosphere that you can bring your kids or have a romantic dinner with the sineficant other.

Your brothers schedules are the same and the rest of the employees like it when you both are working together. Yo two were like a superhero team that made all things happen. Little did they know both of guys had big goals in mind and working on them everyday. You made money everyday in which you liked. With that you really get on some bullshit. You start drinking and smoking everyday. You would hard all hours of the day and week. You had to get out of your sisters house and get your own fast.

As time goes in you start noticing things were coming up missing in the room you were sleeping in. You never blamed your family but something was not right. You didn't even bring it up to your sister because she didn't even want you there in the first place. That bothered you a little everyday. You attempt to go through the process of elimination but it was hard because not that many people lived in the house. People would come over to chill but those who did you never thought they would do things like steal. Everybody was fly so eventually you started blaming yourself. Maybe you misplaced things. It happens. Just said if it wasn't misplaced and it was taken they either needed it or wanted it badly. It is materialistic shit so you didn't give a shit. He who took it is just from the bottle of the barrel and need to stay with the crabs.

You light up a blunt every time you would come home as to enjoying the come up and everyday doing something creative. You stay on the top of your reading and writing. You would chill and attempt to stay focused but hate is in the blood of the deceivers and the smoke screens are in the air and the spread of imitation love is in the air. All these things you know of and use them as a drive to be even more successful in life. With your sister really not wanting your there would weigh on you. You understood why she didn't want you there because when you smoked you were a different person.

One day you didn't have to work and you went to get something to smoke. You would smoke in the room because you were not like everybody else and smoke outside. You liked to enjoy yourself an relax so you smoked by yourself. This was the first time you smoked out of top paper. Wrong move. You were so high you had a blackout and don't remember anything. When you woke up in the morning you seen all the damage that you have done to the house. You literately broke the bathroom toilet. Like who does that and how when it instilled in the floor. Your sister said you swung on your brother in law which was hard to believe but he said you did and the kids seen everything.

Your sister kicks you out of the house. Your mother was so upset she didn't want to talk to you. You were so embaressed you was happy to move out. You did the same shit your sister said you was going to do, cause an uproar. It was time to go. Regardless if you got your shit together or not it was time to go. Your mother puts you up in a hotel because you did have a job so could hold it down and the bus was right on the road so their would be no excuse on why you can't get to work. Here is the next level of life.

Chapter 2

You stayed at your brother Ace house before your mother put you up in a motel. His girlfriend would be on some bullshit because you were there but he was your brother he would not see you on the street at no cost. After a few days she seen that you were actually cool and stopped giving your brother hassal over you staying there for a little bit.

His girlfriend was more relaxed now and began to smoke and drink with you and your brother. She seen that the relationship that you two have would be cool to be around. It was more protection. You was riding with your brother regardless of the situation. You had to emphsize to her that regardless if you were living their or not you would never in a lifetime now or later disrespect your brother. You would never be alone with her just to keep it in her mind that you were there for your brother and nothing else. If it wasn't for your brother Ace you would be on the street with a job. So big up to him. That's real love.

Your mother finally outs you up in a motel for a week while you go back and forth to work luckily you had a job or it would be worse. The whole objective is to stay until you find a room for rent . That would be the next step to having your own apartment or a house.

You worked everyday if you could. You had a girlfriend which was one of your old girlfriends but she would be at work doing 16 hour shifts she really didn't have time for a real relationship. You worked like you use to do on the streets selling drugs. You have good work ethics so wherever you would be, go, or worked for they would get the best of you. A hard worker.

You are now pulling doubles and filling in for those who could not work that day. You liked money and liked to work hard for it. You appreciated it more that way. You earned it and nobody gave it to you. You would still smoke and did less drinking. It made you sluggish. You smoked cigarettes and the hustle. You would walk to Wal-mart for food to put inside of the microwave at the motel. Your girlfriend would pull up in her Buick Lacrosse and chill with you whenever she had time off. That was not many times. You looked at it like things in your life has to get better or going to get worse and failures not an option.

You wine up finding a room for $80 a week in your old hood. That was a come up. You made that in one day or more on some days. You had to move all your things from the motel to the room. Your dad helped you move your things and helped you get an air conditioner. You bought a twin size bed and your dad helped you move it because he had a truck. You were set for a little while with going back nd forth to work until one night it went down.

You came in from work one night had something to smoke feeling good about things. Everyone was sleep in the 3 floor house and you didn't actually see who all lived there because you always at work. The bathroom was right by your room door. You thought you could go take a shower and leave your door unlocked. Bad move. When you got out from cleansing yourself feeling good because you did good at work you noticed you door was ajar a little more than you left it. When you opened it up you immedietly went to check your pants pockets to see was your money still in them. In a state of shock they were not there.

Fools move for whoever took it. This is not family. This is the streets anything can happen when things like that happened. You put on your clothes with rage in your mind and you go knocking on everybody door. You were waking the house. Once again you were causing a uproar in a time where everyone is sleeping. You eventually took it down to sleep. You stayed up half the night because you was bothered but in your mind you was going to catch everybody and who was anybody going to work.

The morning came and you seen a few people some you knew and some you didn't. By the time you start asking questions the landlord came and wanted talk to you about all the banging that was told to him last night from your doing. You attempted to tell him all what happened but it was already in his mind to kick you out. Sucks to be you because you got kicked out once again all within a month.

11

Your girlfriend helped you get your things and took some of them to her house but you could not stay there. All girls house. Your father was upset because you got kicked out regardless of what happened he was upset.

Off to the motel again and this time you had to look for another room in which you found in no time. The room that you found was a few blocks down and you had the down payment to move in right away. It was not far from the transportation center and did not disturb you work travel routine. It was a block and a half away from the liquor store so you was real cool with that. You also knew the tenants and the neighbors so you were comfortable. You had in your mind you was going to stay their until you find a apartment to go to.

The drug you would smoke would be weed and "wet." In California is was called " angel dust" and other places it was called different names. It definetly a mine alternating drug. It was a hallucinating drug. In the books it was a drug that would make a person jump off high building, jump in front of moving cars, and make you strip down naked as if your clothes was on fire. Some drug huh? It was in the category if weed. It was not a hard drug like herion, crack coccain, powder coccain, or any other drug that have a person OD or break into your house because a person spend up their money on it. Those drugs was a no no. Depending on the person it has different effects. You would put it with weed in a blunt or by itself and smoke. At times you would be cool and at times you looked like demon to the naked eye.

One day you did not had to work and you were inside reading and looking at tv when you heard someone getting cursed out. You decided to step outside to see who it was. It was one of the neighbors getting cursed out by her baby dad. In your mind you told yourself you don't get into relationship business but this situation was a little different. You are against oppression and it look just like oppression to you. You sat on the step and lit a cigarette to hear all what was being said. The conversation was all about he would beat her ass and anybody else that would bring to handle him. That was a key.

She was jumping to guard herself from getting hit. He looked at you and turned back at her and said he can beat anybody. It was on. You put out your cigarette half way and got up from the step. Before he knew it you grabbed his lower shorts and his upper shirt and flipped him to the ground away from her. He was in a state of shock. He got up to act like he was going to do something but thought twice about it. You were bigger and in his mind he knew he could not fight. His mother came out of nowhere crying to not hit her son. You respect women so you got back on the step and relit your cigarette that you had put out. He really got loud when his mother stood in between you two. She was saying not to fight but he kept getting loud. You told him to step in the street away from his mother and this time you will put all hands on him. He jumped on his phone to call for help. You stayed cool knowing whoever he was going to call you probably knew them.

The young kids people pull up and he jump in the car telling you he will be back. To you it was whatever. The listen was taught that as long as you were living there he could no longer come around talking shit to his baby mom let alone anyone else.

His mother started to yell at you in the protection of her child. You attempt to explain the situation but in her eyes you were wrong regardless of what her son did. You just look at her baby mom as he pulls off in the car and you asked her was she okay. She replied with a yes and was impressed that anyone stood up for her. She did not know you at all and thanked you. You walk inside to continue doing what you were doing like nothing every happened. In your mind the kid was going to come back at night and you would be ready.

The night came and the kid never came back and you had to work in the morning and had to pull a double. The night was cut short because of work but the word got out about how you handled the situation. Another time you would get into trouble. Does it ever end.

Chapter 3

The day came where work was work. You picked up your tips from the night before and walked away with the tips you made from the morning. At night you had to keep your tips in the stores safe as the night manager had to sort things out. You would tell your brother how things when down. He would just laugh because he knows you have a impulse issue but was cool with it. You only reacted when something got disrespected more or less you. That night was a good night for the both of you. The conversations always went on to how you both can improve each other goals to become successful at doing them.

The night was coming to an end and you both got off work together. As you know people at the job seen you to as powerful pieces together let alone by yourselves. You just followed Ace lead. He was a good leader and you follow good leaders even when you are a leader in your own aspect. You had on your mind that once you got home it was possible he could be waiting with people to jump you so you was prepared for whatever. You showed up at the room on the block and everyone was outside as usual just enjoying themselves. You greeted them all and ask the girl was she okay. Her reply was the same, "yes." You head into the house to take a shower because it was a long hot day and wanted to go to the store to but something to drink. The liquor store closed late and knew you were good.

After a shower you would be heading to the store and asked if anybody wanted anything. Everybody Had their things they would enjoy the night with and you walk to the store by yourself. You get what you wanted to drink and a pack of Newports to smoke for the night into the next day. You did not have to work until second shift the next day so you were going to have a late night.

Once you got back to the house you sat outside with everyone else. The conversation was about what you did the previous night. You was thank by her other sisters and was invited to whatever you wanted but you was cool but grateful as they were as well because you helped their sister. The mother came out of the house. You tried to speak to her but she did not have any words for you. The females was telling you how he would come around every now and then to start trouble but they had a feeling that he would not be coming around anymore and they was right.

The night went smooth and you kept your cool and did not let anything get to your head about the incident. The girl had words for you in which she never really thank you for the rescue. You two talked for a little while the rest of the people who were all there stayed on chill mode.

The daughter of the landlord put the icing on the cake when she gave them a good report about you. Saying you was a good guy and would give your shirt off your back if another person didn't have. That made the new neighbors feel at ease and was glad to have you around. Plus the relationship you had with the people in your city was good as well. They found out that you knew many Puerto Ricans and most of your friends were Rican so they really took to you.

Your female friend came over that night out of the blue. You were in the house at the time just relaxing with your beer and vodka. You answer the door surprised that she even came over. She wanted to stay he night and you agreed to allowing her to stay. You don't see her like that since you two have been together due to her work schedule and your hours. That night you both had sex like it was a long time coming but you knew it would not last long. With you smoking wet and her not liking it, it would soon be over. You had a problem with not seeing her all the time. You knew it was just a matter of time before shit hit the fan.

Th following day you woke up next to her but you had to go to work in a few hours and she had to due the same. Her work hours was two 12 hour shifts back to back at least 4 days a week. When she is not at work she is sleeping. You are not mad because she is a single mother working her ass off but you are not getting the time you want and she can't make time.

She gets up and go to her house to take a shower and get prepared for work then come back to get you. She worked in the same area as your job was so it was cool and convenient for both of you. She would buy you cigarettes whenever she brought herself some. She would pull up at your job and you both would sit in the car finishing your cigarettes and conversation. Not knowing when you would see her again let alone talk to her you exit the car after giving her a kiss. Sometimes it felt like it would be the last kiss you both would give each other.

You step into work with the envoirnment of money and people having a good time with family and friends. You fit right in. You greet the coworkers and clock in and immediately get to work. That's what the coworkers liked about you, every time you came to work you work. Your brother Ace was there as usual. He loved to work hard as well. Hustling is the game and work was a hustle.

You both worked the 8 hour shifts then go home on the bus. You couldn't wait to see the neighbors because they were your company at home, plus they were females. You would have your girlfriend on your mind but you would not see her in days at a time. As you get home and do your routine as far as take a shower and hit the liquor store you chill with the neighbors and whoever their company, your girlfriend pulls up. She got off work early and didn't have to go to her second job that day. She was upset that you was what it looked like hanging with all females. You told her that she knew she didn't have to worry about shit because even though you may hang with whoever you would never cheat. She was not feeling it anyway and you both came up with an understanding that it would not work between you two. End of that relationship. Staying focused you were trying to do and did not need additional obstacles.

You continued to work and in your eyes having fun. People loved your presents and the family loved you. Your extended family from west to the east loved you too so it felt like you were good. Its about you and your loved ones as you seen it. You were apart of what the government called a security threat group. You did not see it like that but you can't help what people do in the past. For all that matter many religions were threat groups as well. You were apart of a movement that was created for peace in the urban area. Against those who oppress and one of the biggest oppressors was the government and everyone knew it. You guys did not cause trouble but was not allowing trouble to come your way or anybody else way that was living right.

You extended family were under umbrella that dealt with freedom, justice,equality, truth, and loyalty. Not all people can live like that. Only a selected few and to other they seen it as a threat. NONE CHYPER! You guys don't live in fear and neither should anybody else live in that matter. You guys did not need the local police force because they were trained to incarcerate the people in the urban area so you were against them. On top of it they were killing blacks. Black lives matter right.

Chapter 4

Young Malcolm X is what you considered yourself as. Your were bought up militant style so you were with the by any means necessary motto. Some people were born to follow and other were born to lead. Every position mattered but at time some would take on more than they can handle because they want to prove something to someone that do not matter or just dealing with pride issues. This is what was going on within your extended family. Big bro was away and their were other brothers that were trying to take his place while he was gone and were not good leaders. You did not listen to those who try to run anything not right, especially when you knew you were one of the best canidates to lead but not run the family. That's where some get it messed up at.

You were still working and doing what you do enjoying life. Their were times when you were called to family meeting attempting to be ran by the disqualified brother. You would come just to present your presents. Not to show you were bigger but you did have love for the family and a silent cannon. You had to make sure things got ran right and everyone was on the same page. It could not get together and some felt the same way but the target was on you. You would tell them that you don't listen to orders by anyone. The only person you were listen to is your big bro. You and him are alike. You both deal with intellegence not brute. Two of your so-called brothers would go behind your back and talk to your big bro and tell him that you don't listen to them only him. That seems right in your eyes.

You would go and explain to your bro why you don't listen to others who can't lead let alone have their own life in order. You are older and have more life experience on them so why listen to anything. He understood and told you and Ace to do your own thing but keep it straight. That way the wave. Be successful in all ways and stay away from bullshit and that's what you both did. Of course other felt the on type ways but you all are your own men with different distinations. Your and Aces distination is way bigger than most. Not all your brothers was against you or Ace but only pushed for it to all happen. That was love not hate. If they who did hate only knew if you were on they were on but men deal with pride and envy which at times turn into hate. It was just motivation for you. You moved to your own tune not others who tunes that don't move you.

You come home one day to your room and you were drunk with something to smoke in your possession. You wanted to get comfortable, relax, and smoke. Just relax in which you did but did not smoke. You were tired from the day and drinking. The morning went to come and you did not have to work that day. You decided to do what you normally don't do and that was smoke in the day time. You were feeling yourself. Maxed out with a job and goals that were bigger than the universe so you thought. You went to the store to buy an empty to smoke out of and blew like you were free as a bird in which you was. Your rent was paid already and you had some me time so you laid back and smoked. What you didn't know is where you had put your phone. You was not worried about it at the time. From what you knew you cam home, took a shower, and went to bed with everything still in your pants.

You grabbed a lighter after you rolled up the wet and smoked til the smoke was all gone. What you did not know was that while you were smoking your mental went to another stage. After the smoke was all gone you decided to take out the trash that you had in the room and do some cleaning. When you took the trash outside you heard some noise on the other side of the fence. The fence had blue tarp on it so nobody can see through it so once you heard the noise you looked up and the faces that you saw recognized you and ran, for what reason they ran and you paid no attention to it.

You went back into the house and started looking for your phone. You remembered that their were a few guys that were in the alley but it was at night time and you didn't bother to think that someone have stolen your phone. That night you looked high and low for it but didn't find it. It was a long night that night.

The following morning you triple checked and you found nothing. You thought of the guys you seen and put faces on them. A couple of guys you never seen before but you knew one. The landlords daughters husband was one of the guys in the alley. As you waited for the morning to start for others, you remembered that you heard a noise that sounded like your phone may have fell out of your pocket and hit the ground. You went back outside to check by the trash can and found nothing. Fiht game was in the air.

You seen the husband a few hours later and asked him if he seen your phone or a phone. He states no but you did not believe him because he gets high and could have sold it for anything. You put up with a little argument but was not going to accept no or he didn't steal it for any reason. A fight began to erupt. In the back of your mind you did not want to go to the extreme because the end result would be you getting kicked out and for sure that is what end up happening.

The landlord was called and the talk was that you were causing an uproar with the husband and without a doubt he believed it and you had to go. You still did not find your phone so it was not over. The cops were threaten to be called so you calm down. Once again you were kicked out of another place within 3 months. The last 2 were Puerto Ricans so they were not trying to hear anything from you going against their people. Luckily you had off that day and back to the motel you go. This time you stayed at the motel for a little while. Fuck this is some bullshit you were saying to yourself.

On your way to work you seen an old friend and one of the home girls. He said was I looking for a job. You replied with yes but it has to e better than the one that you already had in which you was not mad a what you got paid. He told you it was and you would be making a lot of money.

Your eyes go up when he said more money. He gave you the instructions on what website to look up and how to feel out the application. You do so and within that hour after you filled application out you got a phone call from the job. They wanted to send you a link that involved another part of the form. You filled that out and the following day they called you to come in for an orientation. You were surprised at how fast that went. It was only a matter of days you would be set up to work at UPS. A few days went by and you and your mother was looking for another room to lay your head in while you work and get it together.

That Tuesday you had called out of work to make the orientation. You took the long ride by bus up to the job and by the end of your orientation you were hired with a schedule. You told your brother Ace that you found another job that pays more and you were leaving the job you were at. He was cool with it knowing that you were good with employment. You stated work the following day.

Once you got to work you seen that damn near all the employees were from some kind of hood or temp service. It was a mixture of Philly and Jersey in the building all wanting to work and some that did not give a damn. Now this was a place you could be at for awhile and make money. It was mandatory overtime so you know you were going to make it because you liked to work and the only thing you had to do at home was type.

A few days go by and you seen that the job was easier than t looked. All you had to o is sort the mail and send them on a converter belt to get bagged and sent to another UPS warehouse to get delivered. You seen over with time that many people would quit and call out a lot because this one position that put the mail onto the processing table would be a lot of work. Yo started filling that position in which came with a lot more hours. You were working 48 hours a week to 65 hours a week. Check looking so beautiful. Your mother wine up finding you a spot that was renting rooms. She knew the people who had the room available. She delivered their mail. Once again it was on. It was down the street from the public library and on your days off you would very much do so, type.

You wanted to go back to school and you started looking for places to go or will approve you for financial aid. You would set an appointment for Harris School of Business. The classes you wine up taking was not what you were going in for but it end up being a good one. You took up Legal Office Assistant program. Once your financial aid came through and you did very good on your placement test you started the next courses which was in a few weeks. At this moment in your life you were doing good. Have a place to stay, a job, and about to go back to school to further yourself in education. It isn't what you wanted but it beats being locked up or homeless.

The day you was in need and you wanted to deviate because you was doing what you had to do as far going to school and going to work.

Everyday you would make a way to go to work and go to school. Everyday was tired as you went to work and also type up the homework you had to do. The hours you was getting was cool but it came to a point where you had to more hours than usual. As you worked it was coming into play where you could not work and go to school. The hours were crazy. You had to go to work at 5:00 then had to go to school once you were dropped off at the transportation center. Your bus was already waiting for you to go to school.

It was times that you had to carry your bike on to the front of the bus then jump onto the bus with correct change. You would open up your book to see if you had all of the thing you had for school and dealing with the bumps on the road was difficult. Your mind was at work and at school. Once you got to the mall and travel the doors that was automatic you was moving fast just to be on time. As you walk through the mall you would see early morning people walking an jogging the mall doing exersize. You was amazed at the fact that people actually walk the mall before hours.

You still had to keep it moving because you had an ajenda. You would look at people and think like that would be you in the future so you have to keep everything that you were doing in order.

The building is a lot of stories high and you were only only on the fifth floor. You would walk through th doors like you knew where to go. You sometimes would go left forgetting where the classroom is. You would be tire from the night before but you knew what you had to do. The class would be full and at times it would have a few people it in but your whole reason was to get the work done and go home to get some rest.

The day would be new to you. You would go in and set t any computer and just listen to what the professor was say and high lighting things down that she would talk about. It would occur to you sometimes that she was younger that you was. It was a more motivation to do what you needed to get done in school like you was in your younger years. You would nod off sometimes because of work. You had to push yourself everyday knowing what you had signed up for.

He teacher would not say anything to you because she was to busy teaching the class.

The day was real and you could not wait for the day to be over. You was so tired you could not wait for the bus to come and take you home. You got off the bus and travelled to the house where you had a room in. You flipped on the bed and wanted to just go to sleep bad.

Hours went by and you had your alarm set to wake up because you had to go to work. You would grab a little to eat whenever you could. You would then jump up from your sleep take a shower then put on your work clothes and run to the bus stop. The usual. The bus would come and you would get on paying with cash and be slumped on the bus knowing you had to get to work and go hard.

As the ride was long and you would just listen to music on your phone with your headphones in. The bus ride was long and you knew once you got off that you would get it in o the line. As you clock in you would see people not coming to work just because they just don't want to work. You see an oppirtunity to come up on some hours. You grab a locker to put your things in and keep it pushing down the aisle. You start to notice that people awcknowldge you and you give them the hand waves and head nods. You feeling good and you had your way in the work field. You look at those who actually work their. You walk through with a walk like you was going to be their for awhile.

You went to your work area to set up your place and ready to get your hours in. Your station was how you left it and you was ready to go. Another way in the work life is what you wanted to do. It was hot and you knew that the day would be very busy. You held your position and seen that with your work ethics you would go far. There are many positions in the warehouse that you could topple and you would improve your own skills so others who had higher positions can see your work.

Your shift started and you were on your feet. You knew that working faster than the others can get you more money. A raise. That is what the people do go faster and get more money so you moved at a pace you thought was faster than the rest of the people that were in the building. You would process mail like it was no tomorrow. You had ten hours if not more hours to work. The job was work until the job was done. That job would be long and you was prepared do to do what it had to take to get it done. More hours said more money. Even if you had to go to school the next day you worked hard without it even on your mind.

Lunch time came and went. You had to get a way to go to the bus stop and wait for the earliest bus to run. You were tired and the only good thing was that it was a store open to get something to drink or eat for the ride. The bus driver was cool . Back to the basics.

Chapter 5

Time had lapse and you had a test in school coming up. You had very little time to study because of work. You had all your paperwork to go over right before class to go over. Time was up to clock in. You professor hand out the test to everyone to take. It was not long and you went through it quick just to look at the questions. You were nerves and your body temperature started to rise as you start to look over the first question.

You thought about all the movies you looked at and how they were all nerves as they took their test. You went through them all slowly wanting to get a good grade on them and you knew once you handed the test in once you were done it was no turning back. One by one people would get up and turn their paper in and get graded. They had to return to their sets as the professsr graded them and gave them back. That made you even more nerves.

You did not want to rush and did not want to be the last one to turn in your paper. Regardless on when you finished you did not want to be looked at like you were the slow one in the class but you knew that taking your time was important.

You were done and you walked up to the teacher and handed the test in and sat back down to jump on your phone to look at the text saying when you had to go to work today. Every day the start time was different. It depended on how mush mail came in foe the day. You notice that as the week went on the start time was early because of the mail that had to be sorted Towards the end of the week the mail that had to be sorted was a lot. But it was ok, you were getting hours do you were cool with it. The later the better because you had school during the day.

The teacher would grade them and hand them back to all who was finished after she marked them down in her own notes. Some did well and other did bad but no one had a failing grade. The professor called you name to ask some questions she knew you knew the correct answer to but answered it wrong on the paper. You were so nerves even when she asked you the question you had wrong. She would only ask certain questions she knew that you or any other person knew verbally because you or other class mates She did not ask every question on the test that you or who ever had wrong but as you said it was only certain questions age would ask of you.

You would think about the question but would answer it right once she asked you. She just want you or any other person to do good but at the same time she was not going to hold your hand through the entire test.

Once she graded yours she would call your name again and give and the others their paper back and at that time you had an option to leave because the course that she was teaching is over. The grade you got back was good for your first test. You had gotten a B plus. You were happy and could not wait to tell your mom.

You would test you mom the results to your test and she was happy for you. Back home you went and only had a few hours to rest as your brain went into overdrive. On the bus you were cool because your first grade was good after being out f school for so long.

You started to take a liking for a female at work who you did not know had ex boyfriend issues along with kids issues. She did not take to you at first because she was cautious. She did not want to hook up with guy who was only going to be in her life for a short period of time because of her kids and her own emotions as well.

You eventually end up switching you work potions because people were calling out all the time and it was hard to have the potion filled. You took the initiative to do so and it came with more hours but it was a set pay hour. No more how fast you get done pay more. It was a set $12 an hour and you had o come in early and stay later. You were cool with it because your classes did not start until eight in the morning and was done at 3 in the evening. Your work did not start until 5:00 because you switch positions. The old potions start time was a 6:00 every day and ended pretty much at 2-3 on he morning. This potion started at 5pm and ended at 4pm.

You were picking up hours with the new potion you took up but it was starting to affect the time you had to study for school and homework. You would get off late and fall asleep on the bus because of the long hours and would sometimes miss your stop. You would get off at the last bus stop and walk back to the transportation center. Sometimes you had school or you was going to go home to get some sleep to go to work the later an do it again.

If you had to go to school, you had to hurry up and catch the bus and go to school. If you had to go to work later that day you was lucky to get any before work regardless of school or not. You would only go to sleep for a couple of hour and had your alarm clock set to wake up and hurry up and catch the bus to work to work long hours. You be extra tired to where it would affect your work at school. You knew it would be a day where you would have to stop school and keep working.

As you would get paid every Friday, the lady at the house would eventually catch a liking to you. You would give the husband the money and he would give her what she needed for her weed habit and he would go buy himself some crack in which was his habit. He was a veteran of war and was medically discharged for his work and would receive a check every month on top of his fathers diability check to help pay the mortgage for the month. They was getting a nice piece of money every month but with both weed and crack habit they would rely on you for your weekly check.

As time went on you and you relationship with the line leader would elevate. You would come in on the time she would clock in and leave and hour earlier than she would clock out. Timing could have been no better. You was getting all the hours because of her and you would milk the clock just to spend time with her.

The next simister would come where you would take on computer exel for the next course. The professor was the person to teach that course in the beginning but she would stop due to her teaching her other classes at night.

You next professor was also a woman and young. She was a blond haired female and like to hangout like she was still in her twenties. She reminded you of the hippies that molded the race problem that was going on in the seventies. She looked like she smoked weed and was one of the coolest white females you ever seen in a long time let alone reaching college. Her teachings was way easier than your prior teacher.

The long hours at work would still affect you classes. You would start missing classes because of the long hours and would find yourself hooking up with other classmates to find out what was goin on the days you would miss.

You were now in the work field more than you were at work. A problem began to occur when you were taking to another female you were feeding mail to. The only thing about that is that she had a boyfriend that worked their as well.

You paid no attention to the boyfriend because you had a female friend you was talking to and had work to do. You would go back and forth to all the lines you had to do. Everybody who had to load lines were called sweepers. Everybody had at least five lines each to sweep and you would be moving so fast that you would be sweeping six lines at a time. You would be sweating so much that you would losing weight everyday you worked.

Everyday was the same you would come in an hour early to set up your lines you would be working for the day and prepare for the others would worked the lines set them up. You would be getting hours every week and get paid direct deposit every Thursday night. The people would yell out every Thursday night when the money would be inside everybody account and people would go on lunch break to go to the local ATM to withdraw money for the morning and you would do the same to pay the weekly payment you would pay the people who allowed you to stay with them.

As the summer past you were doing fine. You would smoke every now and then because you were working and going to school. You had money and you were thinking of moving out. The friendship with line leader was going ok and the friendship with the female that worked on your line was doing ok but she had a boyfriend and your attention was mainly on the line leader.

Every time you would go on break the line leader would go to the local WAWA and buy you lunch so you did not have to pay for food. The female on the line would be arguing with her boyfriend so much she eventually stop working at the company you were at. That was cool because you did not have time for bullshit and be talking to the line leader and another female at the same time.

A test was up and coming at your school and it was open book test. You kept up with your notes so you knew you were going to pass it with flying colors and you did. You got 100% on your test and you were showing off. Working and going to school will soon come to an end. Time was ticking and you had to choose. Graduation was in February of the following year and you could not keep up because of the hours you were getting at work.

The winter came and you quit school and had on your mind that you were going to go back when you had free time from work. Time never came as the year was coming to a close. The checks were coming in and you were making at least $600 a week after taxes. Life could not have been any better for you.

It has come a time where the relationship was not going the way you wanted it. You would only see the line leader at work and with her problems she had at her home place was getting in the way. The year has came and went and the new year has came. The year opened up good and the old female came back to work. You were surprised to see her as you greet her with a big hug.

Others at work seen it and gossip began to erupt. She came to work with her oldest son and his girlfriend. He seen the way she hugged you and took to you ASAP.

The day went on like a normal day. Your female friend did not know anything about the line leader and wanted you to move in with her. You went against your better judgement and told her you would. She said whenever you was ready she can take you home and get your things packed up to move to her place. She was giving you the keys to one of her cars she owned and you were straight. The next day came and you had it on your mind all night about the decision you were about to make.

You were talking to her the entire time you were at work and played less attention to the line leader. Your new business was the talk of the warehouse. The gossip was how you were a player and the line leader was warned about you but everybody did not know anything about you. It was many rumors going around about everybody business. Relationship and who was fucking who on the job. What was people doing outside of work and what the latest news going on with everybody and all who worked their.

Your name was popping up and you kept doing what you wanted to do because at the end of the day you were single. The line leader was taking it slow and three months has past and still no physical contact was going on between the both of you two. The new female friend wanted to get physical with you and you did not want to do anything with her unless you both was in a relationship. She encouraged you to move in with her and you took her up on her invitation.

Before you left work after a few days than past she told you to leave when she was leaving and she was going to take you to your room to pack your things. It was too early for you to leave and she at least had to wait for an hour or two to past for you to leave and she waited with her son and his girlfriend.

The night came and you were ready to leave. You paid little attention to the line leader and she felt something was going on but she was not going to break her time for you regardless of how she felt towards you. So you made it your duty to leave and allow her to take you home to pack. You did not say anything to the line leader and just left.

Her son and his girlfriend was sleeping in the car until you were done. You clocked out and traveled to your spot at eight in the morning to get your things. As you approached the house that you lived in you thought about how you was going to break it down to the people you were staying with that you were leaving. Once you pulled up to the house you jumped out and just went right inside and straight upstairs to pack your things on a very short notice. It took two trips before the lady of the house finally asked you what you were doing. You told her you were moving out and once Friday came you were going to pay them what you owed them for the week. Little did they know you was not going to pay them anything let alone see you again. On to the next place of your owe. You did not know that the choice you were making was a bad one.

Chapter 6

With your things all packed up in the trunk her you new girlfriends car you thought about was that the best choice you have made. It was to late as you sat back in the passanger set of the car. Looking out the window you would thin about what was you getting yourself into and that you needed a drink for the night.

Your new girlfriend was happy and you did not have to work that day. You were scheduled to have off. It was good that you were off. It gave you time to settle in on the new place you were in. She live in PA and you were fair from home. It was not the first time and not the last.

You pulled up at her house which was a row home. It was not big but it was cool for you. You unpacked and said that you wanted to go to the liquor store to get a drink to allow it to settle in your mind that you were now in your new home with your very new girlfriend with her two grown boys and one with a girlfriend and her daughter. You girlfriend also had a big dog that met you for the first time and it was a little stranger not only to him but for you as well

You unpacked your things and going to play cards with your girlfriend for the night and drink with her. The night went well for all you knew. You had sex with her and enjoyed the fact that this was you new home and you had to deal with it the best way you knew how.

You both got a text by phone on the time you had to start the net day. She gave you the keys to the car you was driving but when you both had to go to work she had to leave when you had to be at work. She was bringing her son and his girlfriend with you two and you would only drive the car she gave you when you two was not at work. You was cool with that but one of her sons did not like the fact that you have not only been given the keys car but to the house as well.

He wanted the car key and felt as though as her son he should have gotten the keys. He was working driving trucks for a career and had time to save up money for a car but thought if he was staying with his mother he did not have to get a car when she had one to give to him. It did not go that way and that's when he would hold over your head that he did not like you and he was going to cause problems with you the first chance he got. More bullshit that you had to deal with. You did not let him bother you because his mother was in the likings of you and he could not say anything about how she handled her business.

The night has came and went and it was time for you both to go to work. That was the most dreadful day because you had to tell your line leader friend that you had a girlfriend and that you was not going to do at the time. You did not know how to tell the line leader and at that time you found out that you actually had feelings for her. At the same time she knew that she was gaining feelings for you as well. You could not avoid her as she was making it her business to come see you as you ere sweeping the lines in he back. She made it her duty to move you to the front of the line where she was so she can watch you as you worked and from time to time you would stop and talk to her when all the lines you had were filled.

Lunchbreak would come around and your girlfriend would take her lunch earlier than you which gave you time to talk to the line leader. This did not go o for long before the line leader found out. She did not want to stop talking to you because you both was to far in. She would still bring you lunch and ask you what would do. Go question because at that time you found out you were in love with her and not your new girlfriend.

At the times you would leave with your girlfriend and would go to her house where you lived and not have sex with her. She knew something was up but did not know what. She would just go with the flow and was cool with the fact that she had a young boyfriend. You had to come up with something because you could not continue sleeping at your girlfriend house and have the line leader on your mind.

The plan was to move out of your girlfriend house and had to find a quick place to stay until things smooth its way out. You and the line leader would discuss a way to exit the house you were now living at. The plan was to get a motel room until the line leader figure out what she actually wanted to do and holding on to you was going to be hard with you at your girlfriend house and not in love with her while she had home issue going on within her own atmosphere. You did not know she was staying in a motel as well with her two boys that did what they wanted to do.

She helped you find a motel near the job and came up with a way to transport you back and forth to work. Going back to school was not on your mind as months came and went. The spring was here and you had to make a move.

You told your girlfriend that the move you both made was a quick move and you had to move out and get your own spot. She could not help you out and it was getting harder for you to stay there and have feelings for another woman. You had your mother to come get you from PA and move into a motel in a small town called Woodstown. It was outside of another small town called Salem City. You were cool with it and had you plan thoroughly thought out this time.

Your mother helped you travel your things from one place to another once again. Times had to change but as long as you was not in trouble and had a job your mother was cool with it.

Time came where yo had to pack your things as your girlfriend turning ex watched you pack up and leave. Your mother was outside of the house waiting for you with your sister with the trunk open. Crazy day for you and you had to go to work later that day. Luckily your mother had off that day to help you if she did not things was going to be hard for you.

You pack your stuff in the trunk as your now ex girlfriend stood at the door and watched you leave her. She did not cry while you were leaving.

You was in sense of relief as the GPS was directing your mother to a motel in a town you never been in.

Your mother pulled up to the motel and you jump out to rent the place that was going to be paid for weekly which was good for you. Once you got inside to pay your get the key to the room the lady that was in charge of the room told you that you had to pay for two weeks. You did not have the money for two weeks but your mother and sister was in the car and you knew one of them had the additional money for you to move in. You came out to the car after telling the woman to hold the room for you and told your mother the situation. Your mother did not have the money but your sister did have it in the bank and it was a local ATM near by.

Your sister was not happy at the fact that she had to come out her pockets on such a short notice but she did. She gave you the next months rent which was considered security deposit and you thanked her. You paid for the room and you took your things up to the room that was located next to the bathroom which was cool.

Once you opened the door to the room you noticed that you had a sink a full size bed and a microwave. In your eyes you were good. You had to work later on that day so you did not have time to unpack your things. You just throw your luggage on the bed with your mom next to you and headed out so she can drop you off at work being as though you were already near your work and you had a ride.

Your mother dropped you off at work and you were just waiting for the line leader to come in so you can tell her what move you had made with her help. You knew she was going to be happy. You only had one question and that was how in the hell was you going to get back and forth to work and to your new spot. The line leader already had that in place and you did not hear about it until she came into work

She came through the door talking loudly so you can hear her voice. She did it on purpose. She knew you would be waiting for her every time she showed up and she like the attention she was getting for you. She was ten years older than you and she was working so much she really did not have time for a relationship but you were different. She made it where you wee closer to her and you both worked at the same place. You were on her mind just as much as she was on yours.

To keep it real you both liked the attention you both was getting rom each other. It was a good chemistry but what fresh relationship is not like that in the beginning.

You told her the news and she loved it. She now had you in her web like she wanted it and she told one of your friends that lived In the next town over to help to out with the transportation. She knew what she was doing and you had no clue but it worked out for you. Rent was high for a week but the hours you were getting each week you did not miss it at all.

Your new friend that your had met at the job lived the next town over and once he came to work he told you that he was going to pick you up at the beginning of the work field and take you home when done. It was a good thing that he was the forklift diver and he had a car because your hours of work ran into the same times as your and your now new girlfriend knew it. She would get to see you everyday and knew where you were everyday. Women.

The work day went on as it normally did and when it was time for you to go your friend would take you to your spot. The day was long as usual but you was not doing nothing else except type you book on the laptop your dad bought you as a gift for doing a good job on your new author career. Thank you dad. A gift that you was not expecting. Things were looking good for you so far in the fear of 2017.

You did not know how things was going to work out for you and your new girlfriend but it felt right and you went with it. Jumping into it fast but it was going on for at least three months so according to you that was ok. Well waiting for. You just wanted things to go good. You did not know what was going on in her background but if she could pull off you getting a room at the motel close to work, a transportation system for you, and more hours at work you only could imagine what she had in store for both of you as far as spending more time with each other. Little did you know all the bullshit she had going on with her ex and the kids and her living in a motel herself and you did not know about it.

Work went well and you were taken to your new spot with your clothes still in the suit case and yo were tired as hell but happy because you were n a better potion than before and in a better relationship.

While you unpacked your clothes your phone goes of and it was you new girlfriend asking more questions on how was the other people that lived in the motel You did not have a answer for her because you just moved In and you did not see anybody all you knew is that you had your own spot again but this time you was not going to mess it up like the previous two. Live and learn right. This time it had to be better. The only thing was that you did not have a tv in the room and you were paying $160 a week. You did not know if it had cable if you was to get a tv or not.

The local convenient store was across the street and you had a microwave and a sink. The only thing they sold that was to your favor is that it sold noodles that you could make in the microwave and ravolis that you would heat up in the microwave and it would hold you over when you were home and not at work. They also sold juice you could make from crash so you brought a juice container so you would have juice to drink. You discovered that you did not have any access to a cable outlet that the motel could have provided so you had to get bootleg DVD movies to watch on your laptop at night on the days you did not work or was up during the day before work.

The only thing was that you were home by yourself while your girlfriend was and you did not like the fact that you were home and she did not have time for you as you wanted to. You was starting to think something else was going on but you did not put to much into it because she set things up for you so you were cool. What ever she had going on will come out in the light if it did not come out in the dark.

You would go to work like everything is cool and people would now reverse the talk on you to on to both are now together. Things are starting to look up and you are wanting more attention and time that she has not dished out yet. Days are going by and conversations between the two of you are getting deeper. She starts explaining to you about the boys that she have and the likings to you may not be good. You are not understanding how she is coming because you have raised kids in relationships that were not yours.

You would be emptying galords as they are filled with work that are constantly coming like there is no tomorrow. Every time you would dump a galord of work into boxes and put them onto a rolling belt that would had to get scanned by computer and placed on a convertor belt to be sorted on the other end of the line to be shipped out to another building to be pushed onto a truck to be delivered to a house for pick-up.

This was your everyday job day in and day out. You had big things on your mind and the world to approach with your ideas. You felt good for the first time in years. You felt like your world was going to explode by the thoughts that's were being stored in you head. You did not think you had enough time to do all what you wanted to do but you also knew that with the time and effort you were putting in one day it was going to pay off and you had to put a time limit on it. Days and weeks could not be counted for. People would listen to you and say what you were trying to accomplish would take forever. That was people words of saying that the impossible would never come. Not to you. In you mine it has already been done two times over by people before you with different dreams and goals.

You would be off in a days t time while working just thinking about the time would come and what you would do with them once they came.

You had found a publishing company that would publish your book for a low price and the person looked at things how you looked at them was so cool you could not wait for the next day just to achieve more. Go hard or go home you understood. All because you had a goal. Somewhere in life you wanted to be and the timing was all on the time you put in to get their.

One day one the job you and your boy was going to walk to the local WAWA to cash your checks and go back to the building to buy some weed from one of the people that was working with you guys until your friend had to open up his mouth to one of the wrong person in the store.

A guy comes in the store and accidently bump into you. He excused himself but it was not enough for your friend. Your friend tells him maybe he should watch his step. The guy had dredlocks and was not in the mode. You excused him and kept it moving. The guy that said something said maybe your friend should watch his mouth. Your friend found it offensive and said he not going watch shit. You told your friend to calm down and that it was not that serious. The other guy decided to say a few words to piss off your friend. You attempt to calm down the situation and separate the two but you could not. You knew that if anything was to happen in the store that the police would be called and you two were going to get locked up because of something that got token wrong.

The guy walked over to the ATM where their were other guys at and said a few words to them. You notice that your friend was not on point with what was going on the store. You over heard one of the guys say that they was in a store and that it was not the best time to get into a situation.

47

You both paid for your food and exit the store. You did not even put two and two together that they worked at the same place you both did.

You kept a mental note of it as you both were walking out of the store. It was the end of the day and you thought you probably would not see the guys again or it was just going to be forgotten about.

On the walk back to the job to go get your friends girlfriend a car pull up in the middle of the road and two guys jump out and approach you two. You both was shock at the fact that two guys who were in dreds jump out of a moving car with the doors ajar in the middle of the highway with trucks coming in the opposite direction and was coming at you two. Straight out of the movies. Real gangstas do shit how they were doing it.

You watched as they both come over the highway and came in the direction of you two saying that if you had words to say it then. They did not come to you. They came straight to him. They went around you and pushed your friend against the gate that covered that over path that was going over the highway. Perfect spot for shit to go down at. No cameras. Mothers fuckers had shit mapped out like they did things like that for a living. Some real Jamaca shit.

As they came to him they were asking what was the shit he was saying in the store. Your friend was not saying shit and he was in a state of shock as much as you were. No words of gangsta came out of his mouth as you stepped in and tried to defuse the situation. The one guy said you did not have anything to do with it and to stay out of it. They were on both sides of him like if he said one word out of his mouth they were going to fuck him up bad.

At that point you were like you wanted to walk away but did not want your friend to get his ass whipped because of you. At the same time you was not offended in the store at the guy so you were actually cool. You turn your back and started to walk away hoping your friend would do the same thing but the situation was over whelming to him and he could not be as tough as he was in the store with the guy at that time. He really did not say anything. With that much pressure in your face and did not know the outcome was bad.

The one guy told him that he thought he was a pussy and jumped into their cars and left but not without saying that they was not from there. That was the icing on the cake because they knew they was not from the same town you guy were but it was not about where you were from it was where you were at the time the situation happened.

They jumped in their car and pulled off like they puled off the greatest heist in the world and got it off. Wow. As they left the spot from you two you both began to continue to walk to the same place because he had to bring back the drink his girlfriend. Not much words was said on the walk and you knew the guys were not going to be at the job once you get back to the building. In the back of your mind you knew you had to see the same guys in the work place as you did.

Once you got back to the building you both did not say much to each other or did not say anything much to his girlfriend in which you both was mutual friends of. You both had a ride to the bus stop and at that time the mutual friend had words for you on the bus. He had time to explain the whole situation to her on his own time and you were cool about the shit. He was mad at the fact that you did not have his back when they jumped out but you were telling both parties to be calm. It all started with your friend opening his mouth about something he should not have.

His girlfriend of course had his back against you but what can you say. She already had in her head that you did not stick up for her man as she thought you would have. You was like he dug his own grave after telling him to cool out so he had to dig himself out of it in which it was to deep. You was the bad guy. Fuck it. It is what it is. It does not stop what your goals are so you keep it moving.

The bus ride was a cold ride but not the last. You were going in a different direction and you had to get off in Camden to do so. You would still be smoking and going to your spot to catch the bus up to Camden was to much commuting for you so this morning you was doing it that way. You was to go to your city buy something to smoke and be back on the early bus out that will drop you off in front of the motel you were at. You had to pay the rent for the week and have enough money to eat for the week. Today was a good was what was on your mind.

You had on your mind that you had to go back to work and see the guys that your friend had problems with and talk to them about what had happened the previous day.

You went to get something to smoke and made it for the bus to take you back home which took you at least an hour to get to. The ride was always ok because you like to site see. Things that you did not see was a good thing. Knowing new places to go was always cool to you and the people that were on the bus was mostly people that were going to or from your city you grew up in to buy drugs or stay their all day high or hustling to get high.

It was very interesting to see where actually people with money who came to buy drugs were coming from. The people that bought drugs in the city where you was from was always from the outer cities that was around you. You knew this from selling drugs in your younger days. Your mind would always wonder on how many people were actually coming from the direction you were going and if it was a sufficient amount of people you were going to start a phone flow to stop the people from going to the city to buy and bought strictly from you but that never happened because you had a job that paid good money. You did not have to worry about police or staying ahead of the game to avoid getting locked up to stop the movement that you had going on.

You get back to when you had a room and stopped at the store to get some blunts to roll up in and get comfortable and get ready for work. You girlfriend was coming to get you for work being as though you both had to be their at the same time and it was not going out her way to much and she did not mind at all anyway. As long as she was with you she was cool with it. Besides she was the one that had picked the spot to stay anyway so that was cool for now.

You get back to the room take a shower then rolled up to smoke in your room while you looked at a movie or listened to music while high on cloud nine.

You would smoke then be in your own zone until you fell asleep for a couple of hours. You wee use to sleeping for a couple of hours and being up for long periods of time pretty much all your life. Four hours of sleep was good enough. Sometimes you slept longer than four or less than four depending hw high you were.

The time came where your girlfriend would come pick you up and take you to work. You enjoyed the ride because it gave you two time to talk about things an work. Hanging with her allowed you to pick up all kinds of hours and the job loved you work ethics so everybody wins.

You get to work and the only thing that was on your mind was seeing what was up with the guys that wanted to fight. You seen one of the guys that accidently bumped into you and attempted to explain what happened but he was totally cool with the event and he insured you that what they were going to do had nothing to do with you and he was glad that you stated out of it because he was becoming cool with you while at work. His cousin was the one that was driving and was cool with you as well. Explained that he also had no problem with you and they did not like your friend because he always was acting tough around his girlfriend. The time your friend acted out was a perfect time for them to show his girl that he was not that tough guy she thought he was and they were trying to fuck hr anyway.

That ended anything that would have gave you problems at the job and started a new friendship with others who was from another town. You did not know that your girlfriend knew them personally and they wee going to be your transportation to and from work. So it was a good thing you did not have a beef with them and became friends with them. Besides one of them was the weed man you later found out and it did not mess up all what was your plans on with your new girlfriend.

Your work went on as usual but now you friend his girlfriend were acting funny towards you because they looked at it like you had made friends with the enemy. Far from it. It was his beef not yours. Fuck it. Mote fiends from out of town and more hours plus you found the weed man. Worked out your way all the way around.

Work went fine and the ride home wind up being one of the guys your fiend and now had problems with you and lived in the town over from you. He was going to pick you up and drop you off on his way to and from work.

As time go on you are digging into what's going on with her life outside of work. She attempt to explain how she has two kids that do nothing but as a parent she has to take care of them. You came across them one time going to work when she came and picked you up. You and your friends would stop at a WAWA and you would see them. Your friend would say that you did not meet them at all.

Your friend knew that she was going in and out of a relationship and you did meet her kids and that she was staying a motel as you was. He would laugh and knew you did not know what her life was like. You would just go with the flow and be cooling as would be in passenger seat looking at who was her children and how she was taking care of them.

She would go into WAWA and grab things to eat for them while she was at work. You was confused at the same time she was going on with her daily life.

Your friend would laugh and just had you the blunt to smoke on a beautiful day as the clouds would just flow with a nice day before had to work. Right before work you would all get lunch for work and keep it pushing. Things was going fine as you seen it.

The days would go as they would and you had a job to do. You would wonder how things would work out with you living in a motel and she was living in a motel in Delaware with two boys and how everything would go into each other. As you would talk on the phone with her, you would hear the kids in the background how they would do things when she was gone off to work. They had a dog that they would cherish forever like a kid. She would give them their food and go to work. The boys would really raise themselves while she was away working hard and trying to establish a relationship with you. You did not know how things would balance themselves out but you was in love with her so what ever the problem was you would be going with it her.

You was trying to be understanding with the situation but she was not trying to let you into her life with them. Something had to give with the situation you are in and the meeting of the boys.

The situation not getting better and the running around is starting to get on your nerves. Every time she would come around it would be about the time you were doing. They were getting in the way of what you were trying to bring to the table.

You would tell her if it was at times you had to be with the kids to meet them. She would always have some type of excuse to not see the boys. The days was getting tiring and you wanted more attention. The only time she would give you was at the job. You took it in and dealt with it until your mother started to say something was not right.

You would text your mother and tell her about what was going on and she would give you advice on relationships. You would take it and use it to your advantage. Your mother was always on you side when it came to anything with her children.

The boyfriend was an asshole and was a drug addict. The boys was taught by the ex-boyfriend that being in a relationship with somebody that was not the same color skin as you it was wrong. The boys liked black girls and the physical parts of the black girl and how they were bigger in certain parts than the white girls. You can not blame the boys because of the fathers up bringing. You think they can change because they are kids but you do not know how bad the wound is.

As the time lapse and the people at he job are becoming jealous of you twos relationships you become the everyday talk at the job. You keep it moving and do not let gossip interfere with the way you both are moving. Eventually things calm down and the gossip go onto someone else. The gossip was about people not dealing with the interacesial relationship that you two were in. She was Italian. Even with her two kids she was still considered a " nigger lover" by her ex boyfriend which of course it bothered you because you were black.

You remembered sitting back and looking at old Italian mafia movies, American Gangsta, The falling of BIG Meech, Franck Lucus, Nicky Barns, Malcolm X, Martin Luther king Jr., and many others and think of how once you get on you was not going to make the same mistakes they made in their movement even though you understood all of their past actions.

Your foundation was built on The Nation Of Gods theories, Freemason teachings, Islamic literatures, Law books, many different languages, Blood lessons, you were an All American. Even though you were not in school anymore your head was still in the books.

You loved to write essays and debate on many and any topics. You were not a Democrate or a Republican. Neither was you a communist or a liberal. You considered yourself as a Nationalist Like Malcolm X once became and by any means you must know and teach the truth and know and understand knowledge is beyond infinite. Learning new things turned you on.

The past leaders fought and died for reasons. They spoke with passion, feelings, and pain. You felt as though it was your duty to keep all those forgotten about knowledge and speeches along with teachings going.

You are now staying in the motel room and paying for it weekly. You feel as though the rent is high weekly but you were getting the hours at work so you did not complain. You now are catching the bus to your friends house because he worked their and it was more convienient for the both of you two. He would drive you to work with his Jamaican cousin and all he did was smoke a lot of weed. You got cool with his cousin as well and after work they would drop you off at the hotel because it was on the way home.

As time moved on you and your new girlfriend got closer. She would think of you at lunchtime and every time she would break you would stack your line and go with her. You liked her style and work ethics. Her car wine up breaking down and her sons father let her use his truck because he did not work at night . Eventually he gave her the truck and he got another car to take to work. They had an understanding because of the kids. When she was at work he would so called watch them and when he was at work she was their with them. She got ahold of the title to the car and gave it to you to hold for safe keepings.

He would do things out of spite with the truck because he knew she was dealing with you who was black. He had a problem with that and it would get in the way of the kids and her using the truck. He became a stalker because he wanted to get back with her but had no chance. He would use the kid as a crutch to stop her from doing things and it would get on your nerves. The kids felt sorry for him and did not want to leave him alone but something had to give.

He was grown and had his own life but would cause problems with her and the kids. The oldest out of the two would think he ran things and it would be hard to get to him. He felt like he was the man of the motel and ran not only his mother but his father. The fathers actions, words, and the mothers actions he was looking the other way. Not a good move for him.

Your girlfriend would start going food shopping for you and eventually you got yourself a single stove top to start cooking full meals for yourself instead of oddles and noodles from the local convienent store. You started spending your money more wisely and she was helping you as well. At the end of the day you were saving money to do whatever you wanted to do.

At work your girlfriend would let people walk all over her and you would feel some type of way. She never had any of her past boyfriends or kids fathers stick up for her. She liked it a lot and with that she fell for you even more.

Both of you two living situations had to get better but before it did she got evicted from her motel room because of her neighbors situation with their dogs. The motel would allow you to have pets but they would just charge you more for the extra pet. The dogs would go outside to use the bathroom but it was the owners responsibilty to pick up the mess the dogs or other pets that you had. The neighbors did not do it so the people who own the property took it upon themselves to put the blame on your girlfriend and her kids. She was not their to take action for it or dispute it so she was the one who got evicted.

She wine up moving in with her friend but that was becoming a problem. The girl would cause problems for the kids while she was at work. It was not enough space for her their so she wine up moving in the room with you and the boys would be at her place. She would go to work at night with you and she would go to the house with the kids. When she was off she would come stay with you and tell the kids she was at work to spend time with you and the kids did not know. It was time she would spend with you without the kids and you two would build the relationship without the kids and she would give the kids time to accept you but you knew that time would run out soon.

Things would be good with you two because you would have time with each other and learn each others ways. She would go to work from your room whenever she had off and when she did not she would go to her friends house and sleep on the couch and would be stalked by the kids father. He would sometime wait for her to get off work or go to work and hit her in the head with his fist or with a blunt object. The would be the part that would get you upset.

You would get so upset at the problems she would be going through with the kids father that you would be like let you go home with her just to catch him trying to do some bullshit and beat his ass. She would disagree with you because she did not want you two to get into it but you knew he was one of those guys that would put his hands on a woman and make her fear him when his was a big bitch and would never put his hands on a man.

You wanted to show her that but she did not want you going to jail because he would call the police on you not because of the as whipping he took but because he did not want you with her and not him. Anyway around he was a bitch and you knew it and you wanted to show her their was no need to fear him. It was just words and physical action on a female that feared a man that hit women. It's a thing that some men would do to women because they actually feared them. Fuck that shit you thought.

You did not like the fact that men would do that to women for their own personal hype. To make themselves feel good. Those guys were the real bitches in the world. The so called tough guys. You and others knew they were the guys that would get locked up and become females or join other organizations to stop the other guys from hopping on their as because they were fake and you knew it.

You both came up with a plan to get a spot wherever was closest to the job. Her, the kids, and you would move into a home and make it a home for the two you. She found a place while the snake you eventually had move next to you were fixing the car. Her and her friend came back to both with pictures that she had taken while walking around the house. The pictures that were shown to you were ok and you decided to take the house. It was a 3 bedroom house with a small backyard. This house was different. When you enter the house it started with the first three rooms then the kitchen and then living room that was connected to the bathroom. It was a great start of a different beginning.

Chapter 7

Your mother helps you both get settled in and now you were on the hunt for more furniture but first you have to meet the kids 5 months into the relationship. You wanted to talk with them face to face to let them know that you were cool and you were nothing like any other male that came into their lives.

You seen them and explained the rules that you live by which are none. The only exception is that no weed be smoked in the living room because it sticks to the furniture and make the ceilings brown and they are white.

The children are not demon children but they are disrespectful all the time and when it comes to their mother they don't respect her either. The one older brother is locked up in prison about to come home soon.

Her kids have to learn the hard way. One son locked up an another is on probation and such a badass he scared to go to jail. His mother is stringing him long by paying his fines off. What she should be doing is putting him in anger management classes to get his anger situated. If she does not get his anger in check he will end up in one of the 3 places: jails, institutions, or death.

You all are in the house and you stay on your laptop typing up things while the house goes up and downs. You still stay in touch with your brother Ace and continue to be a positive influence in his goals and dreams as well as he to you.

You want to go see him at his job with your girlfriend to have dinner. A new experience for the two of you as far as in the relationship. She loved it. It was the resturaunt that you use to work at so the people made her feel comfortable. While their yo both laughed, joke, ate, and drank. A dinner to remember.

The relationship is going well besides her bad children. You both had a job at the same place so the combined income is great.

As the days go on you asked her if she ever been to Atlantic City on the boardwalk or even the Casinos. Her responds was that she have been on the boardwalk in many years and never been to the casinos. You told her on you guys next day off you will take her to the Tropicana, your favorite spot.

You guys set the kid up and off you go. Into the night you go. You drove down their which did not take long. You told her that as long as you both stay on the slot machines all the drinks were free. That blue her mind with that. You both had $30 a piece and enjoyed another memorable night.

The night was so good that whenever we got back to the house we just passed out. When we woke up in the afternoon we ate and went back to bed. My how much fun we had.

The next time we go to the casinos we were going to take pictures so we can start a photo album. Something people don't do anymore.

The kids stayed in their rooms and played their games with no problems. Bills got paid how they got paid. Life was good until the day you totaled the car.

You had to go to court in an area where you know different blacks or/and minorities were not to welcomed. You would be pulled over for nothing and the police will get away with police misconduct. It happens all the time but this time the accident was your fault but how the charges got pressed on you was wrong.

You was coming off of the ram and should have deccelarated but you did not. While looking at the GPS that in your hands guiding you to another exit to get back home, you missed a yield sign and smacked another car. Damn your car is totaled.

You jump out of your car and began to take pictures with your camera. The police came out of nowhere. The officer told you that you can't take pictures. Shit people would not believe you if you told them wat you did to the car.

The officer quickly helped the other driver in which nothing was wrong with him. Of course the officer told him to go to the hospital to get check for injures. In dong so the officer told you that you had to a sobriety test. Fine but why didn't he ask you was you ok. Your car was totaled not the other. As you know the other driver was white. The officer was white. You were black nd they took you to jail.

After several sobriety test done, the officer charged you with Assault by Auto and off to jail you went. Damn one year after maxing out yo catch another charge. Life was good and now the bullshit. You could say what you want about how the charges were being pressed on you but the truth is you should not have been in that area. Back in the county and don't know how you going to get out of this until a miracle happened.

You set in the county and was hearing about a new bail thing that the government started. Bail was no longer going to be given out to people who commit crimes. Once a person is locked up for whatever they did wrong, that person goes to a video conference in which that case is brought in front of a judge and a prosecutor to see if they can let you out on a ankle monitoring program.

For the ones that do not get out on the ankle monitoring program stays in jail until their case is indicted and either plead out on taken to trial. In your case they gave a chance. You were back out on the ankle bracelet that monitor your whereabouts so you will show up for court.

You have no problem catching a bus being as though you have no car now. Thanks to your mother, your girlfriend got loaned a car to get around until you both get another one. Unfortunetly for you, you can no longer drive until you get the new situation handled.

The neighbors that you guys had money because they seen another car. Her grandmother passed away and had a will that said a house was left to her. What see also found out was that her oldest brother had people living in the house and hid them paying rent. Once your girlfriend found that out she took him to court. At court he had two options. He had to pay back all the rent to her or he can turn over everything to her or charges will be filed against him for imposing as a leaser.

She allowed the people to stay in the house as long as they pay the rent to her. With that the rent paid to her it pays you guys rent, so any money that comes in extra in was for bills that were small and no other expenses. You both was good. It was a matter of time before you both get another car.

You was teaching her that even though she has a good heart she can not continue to allow people to walk on it. You was replacing her heart with a wonder woman heart. The things you have learned in books like " 48 Laws of Power", " The Art of Seduction", and even " Laws of Success" will show her how to seek out the negative in people and avoid them if they are not useful

She liked the things that you were showing her. She listened because it was something new to her ears and it can be helpful in her everyday life with or without you. With all that teaching her son still acted as if he was this dude. You told your girlfriend and him that you were going to take him to the neighborhood to see how people live that really think they tough and live in different conditions. Your girlfriend didn't want that. She enabled her sons troublesome ways.

one day you was going o take them all to Atlantic City to show her kids how to have a good time there. He wanted to bring his friend in which you had o problem with. On the way down their the little bad ass son decided to show off in front of his boy and talk shit to you. You were in the passenger seat and that little pussy mugged you in the back of the head. You started to turn around and fucking him up in the backseat, but it was him his little brother and his friend. To much on the highway. Your girlfriend was yelling at both of you. You told her to pull over or turn the car around and take everyone back home.

Once everyone was back home after a unsuccessful trip you were going to fuck him up and if his friend wanted some to, you were going to give it to him as well. It all started over her son sparking up a blunt in the backseat. He didn't want to wait until you guys were in AC. He wanted to do him. Pussy.

You have neighbors who live down the street and would stop past and smoke with the boys and kick it with you. He didn't know what was going on until the last minute. In your head you was waiting for the right time to fuck her son up.

The timing was good and you made your move. You pushed the friend out the way and headed straight for her son. You gave him a body shot in which it surprised him. He started to cry like you thought. His friend did not do anything and his little brother sat back and watched out of fear. That was the first and for sure not the last.

Out of nowhere your big bro called from prison asking you questions about your girlfriends oldest son. Her son wanted to get down with you guys line up but big bro needed to find out all what he was saying is true. It was funny to him that the dude that was all on his dick, his mother was fucking you. The homie. He found it funny as hell.

You was informed that her son was coming home soon and big bro wanted you to keep an eye on his movements once he got home. He also knew that he didn't have to ask you twice. You would tell him how disrespectful his brothers was and you was expecting him to come home to put his little brothers in their place. Little do you know he was a disrespectful mother fucker as well.

He would tell you that his hands are bi-sexual and he don't mind betting a female up. You thought he got that line from someone. He seems like a fraud. Your bro told you to take it easy on him and he seems to be hungry about knowledge. Now you have a ace in the hole dealing with her other sons. Wait until he get home he going to get at them. They think their brother will come home and beat your ass.

The days go on as they do with drama in the house. Your girlfriend is looking for programs that the one problem child can go to once done probation and there are none. He would have to catch a charge to do so. He is almost done with probation and he feel like the shit. If it come down to it he will go with his junky father which is still bad for him.

You don't want the kid going to jail because you know from experience it is a revolving door. That is not the road you want him to go down even though you can see it in his future if his mother is not there to bail him out oh all situations.

If he get into trouble like you think because of the road he is going down he can get some teaching from jail . They have programs he can take advantage of as far as education. He is a smart kid when it comes to school, that you can say. You told him in front of his mother that he does not finish school you are going to fuck him up. You were serious because all that his mother do for him and he let her down. All because he loves getting high that much. The path he on he may become an addict like his dad. You are hoping he change and if you have something to do with that change you with it.

Being as though they are your girlfriends kids you have to try your hardest to make sure they succeed. Plus yo have a good heart and you love kids regardless of how bad they are. Its your job as an adult to guide them on the right path.

The day is coming to where her son is coming home from prison. He will be using your address to come home to but for him it really is rules. That dude is different.

Your girlfriend get in touch with his friend in Elkins, Maryland because he wanted to be the one to pick him up. You both had to go because parole was not going to let him go without his mother.

You had to drive to he court house where he was answering to a charge he had pending while in prison. The judge was giving him probation for the chare but he had 5 years of parole to do after he just maxed out of doing a state bid. The judge just ran it together and maxed him out on it. He was so happy.

After releasing him right at the courthouse he went with his friend so they can go shopping. His friend had plans for him. Your girlfriend reminded him that his parole officer may come past so she didn't idea if he went out of state to stay the night. It would be a direct violation of his stipulations and conditions while on parole.

By the end of the night he was at the house. When he came through the door he felt like a super star. He was feeling himself so much he showed no love to his brothers. It was all about him. He did eight years and came home with no weight like hey didn't feed him at all in prison. He came home with the same mind frame when he was 18 years old. His mind stayed their. He had more game than Parker Brothers. He was a good manipulator by deceiving people. He was heartless.

Before he left prison he was in major debt with other inmates. You big brother cleared it up and told him to follow protocol once he hit the street. He came out and did nothing. The word came back was if he ever step foot back in prison again he was a dead man. He came home not wanting to get a job only to try to get back by selling drugs. Stupid move.

The son is not being understanding of things and he has trouble on the street even though he have not been out on them for awhile. He seen his parole officer and now he is free to move as he please for a short period of time.

The two younger brothers look up to their brother and he is already leading with a bad example. To the brothers his actions just play onto how their own behavior is. You thought time was going to get better but it is not. You just have to keep your composer and go with the flow. However the problem arrive it is what it is.

You now discover that your girlfriend is now pregnant and drinking for her is out of the question. She only smoke cigarettes like they are going out of style. She claims she smoke cigarettes with her kids while pregnant and they turned out to be fine. Whatever. If that's what she choose to do you are going to ride with it. Eventually she has to stop or not.

Your girlfriend and you decided to take a trip to Maryland so you guys can drop off the son. It was a right choice for you because he was about to get into some bullshit in the home front. The plans was for him to stay in Maryland to hustle and come back when he thinks his officer was to come see him. You will see how long that works. You already know from past experiences, its not going to work but good luck.

You are now in Maryland and his friend has a nice set up going on. He has his own business which was a front and he has two houses. His sister live in one house with all her kids and he stay in the other. The thing about the house he stay in he hustles out of the house as well. How stupid is that. You never said anything about it because it was not your set up and never will.

The plan was to have her son hustle for god knows how long and give his mother some money. That never happened. While you guys was there you met the friends sister. She is just as thorough as the brother. She had six kids and they all are cut from the same cloth. The daughter is the smartest when it was about the hustle game. They all knew what was going on. It was like a family business. You wasn't mad at it. They seem like they have it all on smash. Fuck it. If it is not broken don't fix it.

You guys wine up staying the night. The stay was good. They barbequed and had a good time. Like nothing was even going on. They was in a community of trailers. The way they located, they seen all things coming. Meaning cops. The kids were even lookouts and you couldn't suspect anything.

The son wanted to be in the lime light so bad he even had his brothers following him. The one bad ass son didn't follow to much because he was actually scared to go to jail. He just wanted to be down but didn't want to go to jail. He just wanted to be around.

The next day came and your girlfriend and you was going to go back home. The youngest brother wanted to stay there in Maryland. Your girlfriend agreed to let him stay the night. That son was the smartest so she had confidence in that one but the other didn't want to stay. He didn't like the fact that he could not control things around him and he knew he could not give orders by his older brother so he cam back home.

Back home the neighbors was on top of shit. Even though she had a full fledge boyfriend she wanted to fuck your girlfriends son. He wanted as well but he wanted to get his money right first. She patiently waited for him to come back home. She knew he had to come back home because of his parole. She would wait but talk to him on the phone. It seemed like she was in love with him already and they did not even have sex yet. As you said yet. Disrespectful on her part.

In the beginning of their wild was okay but disrespectful. It was controlled by the neighbors girlfriend. She knew hoe to move in situations like this. A professional Whore. Crazy. She liked the thrill of not getting caught and she was right next door. How woman like is that. Luckily the son is not friends with the neighbors boyfriend.

The neighbor played the game so well that she even had her 12 year old daughter playing look out when need be. The son was in the house sometimes when the boyfriend was not there. The girl is only teaching her daughter to mess with different guys and that was cool to have a boyfriend and fuck different guy all at the same time.

The little girls father was incarserated and he was not coming home anytime soon. The little girl did what she wanted to do and her mom had her back. She would wear little shorts in the summer time and her mom would look at it like she trying to be like her. It was cute in her eyes.

The daughter got attached to your girlfriends son looking for a father figure but that was a no go. Through your respect for women you know that daughter should not be around any men until they are grown enough to make their own decisions. Like when they move out of the house. This little girl would go around him in her little shorts and tights like their no pedifiles. You didn't trust him or her.

your eyes served you well. The movement he was making was weird. He was playing both of them. When the mother was not around, the little girl would chill with him and when she was not working the mom would spend whatever time she had with him. It was just a weird situation. To weird to play it close.

Time went on and he gained the trust from the neighbor. He convienced her to let him get $200 and he will flip it for her. She believed him and gave it to him. What he was doing he told the world like he was balling out of control. It looked real good to her eyes. New clothes and all it looked good to the naked eye. He took her money went to Maryland and got low for a couple of days. He only came back to see his p/o then leave again. He played her. This mother fucker even took her car, went to Maryland, ran the toll booth, and denied it all. The crazy part about al that she was she was still willing to mess with him. How stupid can she be.

A little time has past and you are on your same problem shit. Her oldest son wanted to move to Maryland and the little brother realized that his brother was not going to fight you. He mad and trying to find other was to do so. You would just smoke and drink damn near every night. Enjoying life. You would also type up your book everyday. You had things you were doing to make a future for yourself.

It was good going To Maryland for days at a time. The kids had more friends and you both was thinking about even moving over there. The spot next to the friends sisters house was available. Nice as well. You knew how you was, a different environment meant trouble for you with the females. You was not a cheater but something over their would make you leave your current girlfriend.

It was fun at times but you didn't like attention. The things that was going on was very easy to get into and hard for you to get out. Your current girlfriend was with the shit. She didn't know you like the friends sister and you both would talk a lot. Even though she had many kids, you still liked her conversations. You had to go. Back home was peaceful. The only drama was with the bad ass kids and you were trying to break that up. The youngest son would stay in Maryland. He loved it.

You both stop going over there and would enjoy the quality time together with no kids. You would smoke, drink, and listen to music. Life seemed good at the time. Wanted more years like it. You know all good things come to an end. Either in death or just straight bullshit.

Chapter 8

Time passes with back and forth over state lines which is causing a problem with the bracelet people. They are telling you that they have stipulations on you. You are not to go over 1,000 feet from your house and that you have a curfew. You explain to them before you got your address switched out to where you are at now, they explained the rules. The only rule they said you had was to just show up to court, whenever you had it, and to check in every week. That's it. You were on the GPS system. Not house arrest.

While explaining the rules that were laid down to you, they were jotting everything down. They told you all the places you were at in and out of state. Their were places they were not suppose to know where you were going. Luckily they didn't have addresses, only street names. They had you down for leaving the state quite a few times. They were going to get to the bott0m of it but didn't want to get in touch with the original city. They were lazy. Whatever. You will move how you been moving. As long as you do not catch a new charge you were good.

A few days later another problem comes to play. It was not your problem but it was your girlfriends sons. It can cause a problem with you because of the attention her son is causing because he do not care.

His parole officer came to the house unannounced with another officer. You know from your experience when 2 officers or more they are coming to lock you up.

You answered the door and seen vests and guns. Shit you panic but you seen that the vest say parole so you were good. They started to ask questions about the whereabouts of your girlfriends son. You tried to stall them while your girlfriend is in another room trying to get ahold of her son. Luckily the conversation you were having with the officers were outside.

When they ask you where he was, the only quick answer you could come up with was he was around the corner at the Family dollar. She explained how he was not suppose to be out of the house after 6 pm. All you could say is that he just left and it was a quick run and it should not take him long.

She was seeing right through your bullshit. She seen how you were looking at her partner who was looking real good. You started to promote your book and ask if she could look it up and tell you what she thought of it and she did right in front of you. You tried to prolong the conversation knowing that you could not do it because he was so far away.

The officers waited for 20 minutes and started to explain how they knew he was in Maryland because of a ticket he got for running the toll. You thought about it real quick and said to yourself, how did they know he had a ticket when it never came in his name nor did he get pulled over. The only thing you could think of is the neighbors boyfriend called parole.

The officer got frustrated and told you to tell him once he get his ass back in the house for him to call her right away. You responds was ok. The boy is fucking up already and he just got home.

The boy is out of control. You believe he was already like that before he even got locked when he was young. The other reason you let him stay as because he did not have anywhere to stay and they would have given him placement. You should have went that way. The way he talked to his mother he has no disrespect. He felt some type of way because she did not do much for him when he was locked up.

The boy fell to realize that his mother has two different brothers that she had to take care of along with life itself. He resented you for a little because she is now with you and she is getting money. He is upset at the fact you were getting the money but he tend to forget you give her money as well. His whole mind frame is messed up and you hope he would not have to go back to prison to get it together.

He came back from Maryland and the parole officer told him she was not coming past an let it be his warning that if he violate curfew again he will have big problems. Now he stuck at home. He is somewhat cool with it because the neighbor still want to fuck him regardless of what he did. In this token his ex girlfriend from many years ago found him and now want to claim him. More problems to come.

As time went on he got more involved with his ex that now turned into his girlfriend. You were going back and forth to your city to deal with this problem with the car accident. They were offering you a 4 flat. Please not on your worst day. They were waiting for the urine analyses to come back so they can have concrete evidence. Without it, its up in the air. The case is on your side as of now. You would see your brother and he would say how the deal with Atlantic Records might indeed happen. You were happy for him.

One day you decided to take the two youngest ones to the famous flee market. You put some money in their hands and let them get whatever they wanted. You wanted to show them how it felt to have fun with you and to remind them that you were still cool. You are just doing your parenting skills just like they will have to learn to do once they get their own.

The shopping went good. Your girlfriend was happy that you came in the house with things for her. She hasn't a man do much for her but give her problems. You showed her different. She liked the things you brought her and was glad you took the boys out regardless of what you guys were doing.

You reminded the boys that if they continue doing good things like that can happen but if they continue to act out, you were going to get some boxing gloves and show them a ass whipping.

As you figured 2 weeks later you and the kids go to Walmart to get some things and of course the boxing gloves. You also got Monopoly to play a long game. Now that the brother is their all they want to do is play the Xbox in the living room. You wanted to make it a family thing.

The oldest son is doing good with his old girlfriend from years ago. They are now in a full fledge relationship and he is now playing step dad. Maybe that's what he needed or not. The girl liked the fact that he was a bad boy and was attracted to his style. She lived over in Philly. She didn't mind coming over to see him. She even bought him a queen size bow up bed. Whenever she comes over to see him se stays the night.

They came in one day and you just so happened to have the boxing gloves out because you were playing with them. The oldest seen that they were out and wanted to show off in front of his new girlfriend. He came in the living room and put on the boxing gloves to play with his brothers. As he put them on he start talking shit to them. He pissing you off because he was indirectly to you.

He started hitting the kids hard. The on brother attempted to kick up but didn't do much. The youngest ran from him. Once he stopped the brother gave in. Of course the bad ass son said for him to put them on with you. You honestly didn't think he will say he up for the challenge. You put on the gloves with him told him and the boys that the first round was on them so they can go in like they want if they could. The second round is on you and it was their time to see what they would feel when somebody fights back.

You two began going at it. He was doing his best but when you started laughing as he hit you he got madder as he swung. His little son was watching and began to go towards his mother but took the path behind you challenger. As you swung hitting him in the face, as was taking a step back he tripped over his son which caused him to lose balance.

You took a step back and looked on his face. He not only felt embarrassed but violated. He jumped off the blow up bed with a fury on his face. You seen the look and seen how the way he got up. You threw your guard up and watched him get up and was swinging a hay maker. You allowed to hit you while your arms was up blocking the impact. You was taking steps back just so you don't use lose balance. You did not see his step son behind you. As you were going back you lose your balance because you did the same thing the challenger. As you were falling backwards he decided to take advantage of the situation and hit you on the way down. You leg got stuck under you and it hurt like mother fucker.

From a view it was an illegal punch and from another view it looked like he knocked you down with a knock out punch. He began to praise his victory by telling his brothers he told them he was going to knock me out.

You got up and limped to the room. Your knee was at it worst. You knew that he was going to praise that forever. You drank some of you beer and put back on your one boxing glove. You hopped back out to the living room and was surprised that he still had on his gloves. You told him that he took advantage of you tripping in his step son and that round was on him, now its on you. He trough his guard up and he swung but this time you dodged it. You swung fast. He didn't know what to expect. He started moving backwards but you kept it coming. You worked out so you did not let up.

With his back to the wall you unloaded on him. He didn't know how to block and what to block. You told him before that you were fast with your hands. You now proved it to him. One of you hooks sent him falling to the couch. It was a knockout punch but you was going to take advantage of him like he did you.

You started to hit him with some Mike Tyson blows. If a person ever seen Mike Tyson fight it was amazing. He could not take them and gave in. He said you can not take advantage of a person when he was down.

You let him get up and said was he ready for round three, he said no. Job well done. It was in front of his girlfriend, mom, and both of his brothers. You watched him take off his gloves and you took off yours. You went back into the room and wrapped your knee up in a ace bandage. You guess you know how it feels to sprain your knee. You knew it was not the end of it but it will do for now.

A couple of days past and the neighbors boyfriend came to you and told you that the oldest son is going around telling people that you got knocked out by him. You were shocked at first but didn't really play on to it. You told him how it happened and laughed at the rest of it. You knew one day you will have to beat his ass for real. He is the type of child that learns the hard way.

One day the son and the girlfriend was out shopping. You lock the door every night at a certain time for safety reasons. Her oldest son came home and he realize the door was locked and he didn't have a key. You are in the kitchen with both of the neighbors and your girlfriend all talking.

A terrible bang came at the door. You went to the door to open it up. He came through the do with he was the man of the house. Boy tripping.

He came straight down the hallway yelling at his mom, telling her he thought he told her to not lock the door when he is out. You looked at him with a look saying to yourself that is going to be the day you whip his ass. He told his mother in front of his girlfriend and the neighbors that he has to tell her again he is going to fuck her up. After making that statement he then turned to you and said if you have a problem with it he will knock you out like he did when you both was boxing. He is so showing off in front of others.

You asked him if he wanted to go at it now. His responds was bring it on. You told your girlfriend to go get the gloves. This mother fucker had the nerves to say don't go get them, he wants to fight without them. Fuck it he better be going hard in the first round because you are. You looked him and he got into a fighting stands but your girlfriend jumped in the middle.

The neighbor grabbed your girlfriend and moved her out the way. He wanted to fight him as well but he was scared of his bark. You started to walk towards the son. His guard was up ready to swing once you got into reaching range. He swung and you dodged it. He swung again and you dodge that one as well but this time you grabbed his shirt and swung him against the wall. You did that t take him off his stands.

You started punching him in the face. He put his head down and was swinging all wildly. He might have hit you once in the forehead but was taking all the punches from you. As his head was ducked down, you started giving him uppercuts. You grabbed his shirt again and swung him into the microwave rack. You are blowing his body up. He could nothing but block whatever he could.

You finally picked him up and slammed him on the floor and put him in a submission hole in which he gave up. Game over. You let him up and stood there just to see if felt embarrassed about what just happened and wanted more smoke. He did not.

You went to the room and grabbed the keys and jumped in the car. You had to vent so you went to the city which was 30 mins. Away. On the way out the door you heard glass breaking. This fucking dude kicked the glass cabinet door.

You came back to the house and isolated yourself in the room and smoked. You had some beer and vodka left and that was your night. No fucking or anything, That night.

The next day was a little different. You got the respect from him and his brothers. They had a different plan. Get somebody to beat you up.

A few days past and you had to go to the city for court. They came down on the offer and said 18 months state bid is suitable. Not to you. You rejected it and knew they didn't have any evidence to support their saying. You bought something to smoke and back home you go. You was on the bus home this time. Its an hour ride. As long as you had a way back home you were good.

That night you were drinking and you and your girlfriend were arguing. It went on for a minute. It was so loud that the neighbors came over to see what was going on. When the door opened you went into defense mode when it came to others outside of your family.

You started arguing with the neighbor because they don't know how to mind their own business. Your girlfriend jumped in the middle and you mistakenly pushed her. Once you notice that you did they, you laid down your defense system and looked at her. She took a step back and threw a punch. When di not see a reaction from you went you hit your chest, she swung 4 jabs at you. You took them and made sure none of them hit you in the face.

The argument kept going on and the neighbor decided to call the cops when you guys went back in the house. Another knock came at the door. When you opened it up all yo seen was a few people dressed in dark clothing. You shut the door fast and was about to g to the room and grab you knife. The knock came at the door again before you made it to the room.

You opened up the door again and started swinging on the person that was in front of you. As he stepped back you stepped out of the doorway. You seen a few more guys. You looked to your right and seen another victim you felt like he or they was their to hurt you. You started swinging on him as well. Once you turned to swing again on the guy in front of you that's when you noticed that a word was written across his hat. It said POLICE.. Oh shit. You dropped your hands to show you were not going to swing again. Bad move.

One of the officers grabbed your waste and picked you up and slammed you on the porch that was total cement. One of the officers pulled your arm to put it behind you back. He attempted to grab you other arm but you resisted. The officer told you to give him your arm. Your responds was if you give him your arm he will not try to break it. He didn't want to hear anything. You told him again and then gave up your arm.

After a little resist, the officer stomped on your shoulder to try to break it. You workout so it would have to take a little more than a few stomps. You got picked up and placed in the car. You thought you were going to the jail but instead they took you to the hospital because your face and nose was bleeding. They to make sure they did not break anything.

While in the hospital one of the officers was asking you what happened and why you were punching all on the police. You told him in front of your house you have no light to recognize who is at the door. You opened up the door after having a huge argument with your girlfriend and the neighbor and thought they were coming there to jump you so you opened the door up and started swinging not knowing it was the police.

As one of the officers was walking past he was saying how he should have broke my arm. You was responding back telling him how he was made because you was hitting him with a flurry of punches. He got pushed on and he was mad. The officer that was talking to you had to restrain his partner in the hospital because it does not look good from others who are standing on the outside. The results were the officer taking you home and not to jail. They came to the house unannounced which caused the fight.

As you pulled up to the house and got dropped off you got the officers card just in case the others come back to start shit with you and justify it with whatever they want. You walked in the house and your girlfriend was surprised to see you walk through the door. You took a shower and got right in the bed. The night was a messed up night for you.

When you got up in the morning you had more problems than you thought. You tried to get up but your shoulder that they stomp on was damaged. You had a pain that was so bad you had to go back to the hospital. They damn near knocked it out of place. The people in the hospital from the night before. The result was you leaving the hospital in a damn sling. You were fucked up. They got it. Shit as long as it did not end up with you in jail you can take it. Now you had personal beef with the officer that stomped on your shoulder.

You are now home with a story to tell or it was already being told that you took it up top on the police and your shit was fast. The police was so slow he couldn't even defend himself. Fuck him. The fight from your girlfriends son was over and now the talk of the town. Some knew you and some did not. It is what it is. You still wanted a fair fight with the officer. You knew you would not get it but it could happen because you knew the lady who ran the boxing gym.

You was going to prepare a legal fight and the city was going to hear about it. You thought that it would not work because if the city really heard it was going to go down between you and the police would not be a good look for law enforcement. Everyone would want to fight the police, in which they want to do anyway.

One morning the officer was at the gas station store because he went their to get coffee in the morning. Your girlfriends son decided to to tell the officer that you were talking shit about the fight and vow to get him back. This mother fucker want you out the house bad. Funny how people roll. He tried to get you into trouble.

You seen the officer at the gas station and he seen you were in a sling for your shoulder. Now you have to downplay the whole situation because the oldest son fucked it all up. The officer found it funny that you was fucked up but he also knew what you did to his fellow officer.

A few days lapse and it seems like your life is getting out of control a little bit. You are smoking more and drinking every night. The argument that happened that night still did not sit well with the neighbors. Some how some way the temp tags on your car were gone and the only ones that were outside was the neighbors and their friends. You blame them. Its only right. Nobody else fucked with you but they had some type of vendetta against you.

Not to log after that the whole thing started to fall through. You girlfriend said she lost the baby but got pregnant again fast. The people I the house of your girlfriends stop paying rent which put you got back in your rent. The car note was not getting paid and eventually they came and got the car at night. That was another down fall. You came up with a plan to sell drugs from one of your friends house who already had a house flow so it would have been easy to flip your money.

After your girlfriends son heard about what you was going to do he wanted in. You told him you have to see how it goes first then you will put him on. You knew in the back of your head that he always fuck up money and spend the profit and your money or anybody else money. He fuck every bodies money they put in his hand. He not messing up your money and nothing happens to him because he is your girlfriends son. You just led him on to believe he was going to get on.

You told him what the plan was and why you were doing it. Not because you can but bills are getting backed up. He wanted to go to the police station to file identity theft because he wanted to see if he could get cable turned on in his name when him and his girlfriend move out. It had to be on comcast record that was the case. You told him that he can do that after you get back from picking up what needs to be picked up and that was the next day. He agreed.

The next day comes around and through the day you have been making sure shit was going right. You was going to make your move at night when dark and you were going to meet your brother in the city and he was going to spend the night at your house. He just signed a rap deal and you both was going to celebrate the night with you. You with it.

Night fell and you were off. Your girlfriend calls you on the phone and tells you that her son made the move to the police station to file a complaint and that they were going to come past and talk to him. You were pissed. He was not suppose to make that move until you finished making yours. Asshole.

You snatched up all what you were going to get, found you brother, got some weed, and you both had to run to get the bus. While on the bus your brother had a liter of Amsterdam and a 24 oz. of beer for both of you to start the celebration. The ride was long and it was fun You got to the house in a hour and when you stepped off the bus you realize how you were feeling.

When you step foot in the house the heat hit you hard. You were looking for the son but he was not in the house. Like 5 mins. In the house a knock came at the door. Your girlfriend opened up the door and it was the police. You were drunk and needed to slow down. You came stumbling down the hall and your girlfriend stops you right at the door. You slipped a little and started to turn around.

The officers remember you and asked you to come back to the door. You respectfully declined. You started to walk away again and this time the police walked in the house and tried to grab you to bring you out. That's no probable cause. They came their to look for a specific person in which that person was not you.

You fought them off not remembering that the drugs were still in your pocket. As you fought them off in the doorway of your house they smelled a familiar smell. They slammed you up against the wall on the porch and searched your pockets and found the drugs. The son was just so happens to be walking across the street at the time of the arrest. It seems like it was a set up. You were going to jail with possession of CDS. Damn finally caught on some drunk shit. This mother fucker set you up. Damn.

Chapter 9

In the back of the police car again. Entering their jail was different. The process is the same and they get you on the phone as soon as possible. The process was not long to do the paperwork and put on some clothes. This is what you know, you go to court in the morning and their was no bail. Another episode of bail hearings.

You got put in a turtle suit. Fucked up. They can put you with the worst of the worst mother fuckers around and survive but don't put you in a damn turtle suit like you crazy. That process is if a person come into the jail drunk or high on anything, that person has to be seperate from the others. You was different and you need to be treated like a regular person. An inmate.

You sit in a damn turtle suit awaiting for the morning so you can go to court. The room is full of others who are going through withdraw of drugs they put in their system and it was cold. Under the turtle suit you had nothing on. If you have to stay their, everyone have to see a doctor that will approve of them and you to go to population.

The morning came and you had to see the judge to discuss why you feel as though you should be let back out. The public defender showed you countless violations of you on the bracelet. The prosecutor is arraigning for you to not let you back out. Damn they got your ass but you will see if the public defender will fight for you.

In front of that judge the prosecutor told the judge that you violated the bracelet 27 times. Holy shit. If you violated something that many times and did not get locked up, it wasn't that serious. The prosecutor just brings these things up to create a pattern to show the judge if he allows me to go back out to the streets I will violate something. The judge denied your argument. Now you have to stay in jail and your girlfriend is pregnant. The kids are out of control and they are glad to see and hear that you got locked up.

You couldn't get to the phones because it was a time frame because they did not want any other person if they had a infection. It feel fucked up for you because if a person was in there like that you the one that has it with him.

You was in this situation for a week. You didn't make it to the regular process as far as person that come in sober. They had no reason to keep you any longer so you had to leave. Put on some regular clothes that they give every person coming in to their facility. You then was escorted to a unit where it is considered it the intake unit. You rules are basicly the same as the county where you were from.

The only thing about the intake you can stay out and use the phone as long as you are not locked during shift changes. You were on the phone all the time telling your girlfriend the reason why you feel like you do about it feeling like set up.

The food was different and you was wondering you were going back to prison because of your actions. You was just wondering how you was going to do the little jail credits to what you are going to have to handle. The thing that the officer was on the unit with you at all times.. The outside rec. was on the unit but outside. Crazy. There will be no movements.

After only a few days in intake it was time for you to go to population. You didn't know what to expect. Town different and you haven't live there long enough to know a thick crowd of peoples. You was you, you. You could fit in anywhere you go.

Once you got introduces to the other officer then you got introduce to the room you were going to. You put your things away, made your bed, and off to the people on the tier.

You seen some people that you knew from your city, so you was cool now. All it did was give you some body to talk to until you know others. It would not take you long. You play chest, cards, scrabble, workout, shit you good. The day went how it went and it was time to lock inn with your new cellmate.

Your cellmate was cool and its funny because you heard of him and he knows you big bro. He gambled so he had food all the time and you had your own so both of you were good. The stories was crazy and he jail hard as shit. The unit knew who he was and you were cool with him made you fit right in.

The next morning was new but it was just like they did when you were in intake. They call you out to eat. The officer tells everyone to stand in a straight line until he feel as though he is ready to serve you guys. The officers in this facility are very controllive. They like the fact that they can tell you guys whatever they want if you do not comply you will go to the whole. The officer tells you guys to start serving the food and all you had to do is sit at the table the officer tells you to. You should be able to sit where ever you want to. Not in this county. It's a total control issue.

While sitting at the table, you are not allowed to talk to others or give any food you don't want to another. If you are caught giving any of your food away, you are told to empty your tray, regardless if you are finished or not, then go to your room. Not following directions. The county is some bullshit. The officers remind you everyday that the county is not ran by the inmates. It is ran by the officers. Fuck the county but you are their for god knows how long. Adjustment you can do well.

The day went on and you call your girlfriend. She says put money on your books so you can order things once it is time to order. She is holding you down as far as being locked up. You don't know how she is getting money for that and pay bills but she is doing what she has to do. The kids think they run the house while you are gone and she is already tired of it.

Ur girlfriend says how she is getting big and going to the doctors help her stay on top of her pregnancy. You have no choice but to believe her.

She says when the baby is due and you are trying to get all this situation wrapped up as soon as you could.

The public defender come sees you to hear your side of the story. He tells you that if it happened like you said it did you have a huge chance of beating the case. The public defender is going to actually fight because it seems like your rights have been violated and he will do his best to fight the case. He is waiting for you to be indicted then he will take the next steps in filing any motions if any is required.

You go back to the unit and think about your case and who it you are being represented by. You talk to your bunkie because he wasn't playing cards at the time. You discuss what the lawyer was talking about and his thoughts and answers to be of the same as you. You felt good and you jump on the phone to tell your girlfriend. She did not to much about the law but she knew that they was wrong and the way they went about it the wring way.

After hanging up the phone you felt good and you knew that was going to be a restful night. Your thoughts was with a little law library you was going to walk out the door with something light or nothing at all. Your day went on all the way to bed. You could now sit in jail at ease because the major case is about to ne no worries.

The days went on and it was a matter of time you start working out in their gym. You knew that with some pull ups your back can get wide. You started doing pull ups with a guy that looks like he was down a while and use to workout. You routine consist of him becoming your workout partner.

Now you have a normal routine with you studies in law. Luckily you knew some thing about law because of you previous times you been locked up.

Your days went on as so. Eating in the morning; going to the law library and studying at the same time; eat lunch; workout; shower; and bullshit around for the rest of the night. You played chest and dominos one the second half of the day. You even decide to write another book and by the time you were finished, however long you were going to be in there for. You were their to get you weight up, beat the charge and come out with another book. Three stones at one time, you were with it.

Your time went fast and there winter was here. It normally do not bother you because when you do bids, you do them by yourself. The only person that really helped you all the way through any of your jail time was/ is your mother. This time was a little different because your girlfriend was holding you down.

You workout everyday and gain new friends. There are people from Camden but you didn't mess with them to much because they are on some shit like us against them and you not with that. They were cool but you cool with everybody and starting a war you not with. You would read the newspaper every morning and chill with the older guys. They were on some shit like you was, fight your case.

It was time to order your food for the week. The thing about that is you can order every week but you would have to keep money on your books and you think that will eventually be a problem. You order smart.

The cosmetics the ones that's the most money but that's a one time thing and after that its all food which was cheap.

Your order came and it was really time to get your weight up. That's all there is to do. Being locked up sucks ass. The shit is a waste of time on a persons life and you vow to not get yourself in that situation again but there you are. An inmate again. It doesn't break your mold and you just build.

You gained a few associates while your short stay. Every night everyone makes themselves food to eat for the rest of the night. It is called a HOOKUP. You know how to make your own meal but with a group of others, the meal can be way bigger. The people that are in the meal has to bring their own food. Everyone brings their own part of the meal depending on what is going to be made.

The meal is done and everyone eats like it is a home cooked meal. The unit is quite and everyone enjoys a meal watching the game or any episode of their favorite television show. Some kick it with the officer, depending on how cool the officer is. Some play cards and enjoy conversation with each other about females or old war stories. The night ends with a full stomach and more thoughts on how you are going to beat the current case you have.

Several days past and you work hard on your case. Crossing all the T's and dotting the eyes. You continue working out your physical was a must. You were going to come home bigger than were before you had got locked up with the case.

The one assualt by auto case seems like you are going to wear that case but still have your doubts about the distribution case. You seem confident about winning the case but the prosecutor never plays fair. They did not know about you and you have a good public defender who is playing like a true lawyer.

Your girlfriend is saying that she is now pregnant with two babies and she is due sooner than you thought. It was now the spring time and you got offered drug court and you were thinking about taking it. As long as you were going to take it and make it home by the time the babies were born you was cool with it. Now the game has changed and now fighting it is now in question.

You talk it over with your girlfriend and she with whatever that will get you home faster. She knew that if you were going to win the case you would have to sit a little longer. She didn't want that so she came up with a way to alter your mind. She couldn't waste more time at home without you because the bills and the landlord acting like a dick plus the kids that are disrespectful.

It is a crazy smell in the house and you knew it was coming from some kind of sewer system. The smell was awful. The landlord had to find somebody to look at the pipes under the house. They were backed up in which the smell is coming from. The landlord is so cheap that he didn't want to pay the extra money out to get it fixed so he had the neighbor to fix it and he will take money off his rent. The neighbor agreed to it. Why wouldn't he? He fixed other houses on the side for the landlord so fixing the pluming will have them pay nothing for rent.

Smart move if the neighbor was a actually putting in the work to fix the pipes. Both houses are connected so both lines are backed up. The smell is only on your house side more. The neighbor really didn't care. As long as you were out the way all was going to use your girlfriend for all she is worth. Her good heart. That is of the reasons why she wanted you home. Nobody asks like that when you are home because the know you will flip out if you knew someone was disrespecting her in anyway.

You see you public defender and ask him to put in the paperwork for drug court and he did. His advice was give a little more time and he will have the case beat. The pressure was on about the baby situation so you was going to try it. If it works you home if it doesn't you have to work a little harder when time comes.

About 2 weeks go past and you got a visit from another public defender. She was from the drug court office. She came to tell you that you were denied drug court and that she just needed a lot bit of information on you so she know how to prepare your appeal for the reversal of the drug court decision. Finally a feeling of a little peace of mind.

You go back to court in the city where you were from and they found evidence against you. It still didn't affect the case to much. All it meant that you were going to wear the charge in which you were going to wear anyway. Just the thought of how much time if any. Whatever it is you could handle it. Consequencetial thinking is kicking in. A field you have a problem with. You tend to make the wrong decisions.

While waiting for the appeal to come back you still work on your case and get even more upset at the fact that the work at home is not getting done. The neighbor cut a huge hole in the floor to get to the pipes and insects were coming up all the time. The smell got worse and the only thing he had to cover it up with was 2 plywood boards. The job was looking crazy and a big playout to get you back from the bullshit you gave them.

The appeal court date came in the mail at the same time your public defender was telling you that he could beat the charge. You was weighing out your options in which you only had 2. You either sit in jail and get the credits for whatever you was going to take for the assault by auto while fighting your drug charge or you could take the drug court program and go home that same day you get sentence. You eventually choose drug court.

The day came and your drug court public defender was fighting the appeal. They denied you because of a gun charge you caught 19 years ago. She fought well and beat the appeal. The prison alternative was a 4 flat only because of the other charge you caught. Later you walked right out of the jail after 3 months. You came out way bigger than your were before you went in. The only thing that was on your mind was how the neighbor was doing your wife and the house she and yourself was living in.

You walk right in the house and the first person you see is the neighbor in the huge hole in the floor of the kitchen. He looks at you with a smile on his face. You greet the kids that were in the house nd then turned your attention to the hole in the floor.

The neighbor had a smile on his face but once he noticed that you were not smiling he acted like he had work to do. He knew that with you being home you were going to push the issue of the house getting fixed. Come to find out the clog came from countless tampons getting flushed down the toilet. You don't have any girls but the neighbor does. He has 2 girls. Well now the whole must be fixed and you were going to make sure of it was to be fixed asap. Like now.

The night went good with a couple of beers and a couple shots it was on. Sex was in the air and your girlfriend knew it. She had a couple of shots and the night had gotten darker. The kids went to their rooms and you was waiting for your girlfriend in the room because not having sex for 3 months you knew you were going to tear her pussy up.

She came into the room and seen that look on your face and knew what it was. She shut the door and locked it. She even wanted the dick. She jumped on you and you both started kissing hard. You both was drunk and both clothes came off fast. That night everyone heard her. Even the neighbors.

The next was like an adventure. You had to see your officer so she can break down the does ad don'ts. You had to go to IOP 5 days a week plus N/A or A/A meetings 3 times a week. On top of that you had to go see drug court once every Monday and probation every Thursday. Shit you had a lot to do.

The program did not worry about you not having a job. All they was worried about was you doing all what they ask you to do. Fuck financial aspect of things. Its all about their program, damn your life. You have none on the program.

You went to the IOP as required and it was lovely. Their were so many females you loved going to the program. Their were more female than guys. Even the counselors were females and the director. Heaven.

You was not an addict to drugs but the stories you can relate to. Some of the stories you here at the programs would surprise the hell out of you. You liked going. You met new people from different areas and different cultures. Shit was cool and you liked learning things new so you were cool with it.

Every night you drank. Being on the program did not stop anything. As long as they thought you had a drug issue they would never test you for alcohol. So you thought. Shit do catch up with you. You begin to ask questions about the time you would do if a persons urine comes up dirty. The answer was a day or two in jail then let back out. Shit you got that. Vodka it is.

You have been doing good for at least 2 weeks and the hole gotten filled in and the program decided to take a urine from you and send it out to get tested. The reason why they send it out to the lab to get tested is because the cup test only tests for a few things and the lab tests for all things. Even the thins that are not on their paperwork.

You knew in a week you were going to have to do a day or two. The day came where you got the phone call and your officer told you that you had to turn yourself in to do 4 days. You were shocked because what happened to one or two days. You just shot up to 4 days and it was only alcohol. You guess if it was cocaine or heroin the judge or the team would have gave you a slap on the wrist.

Back to the county you go. You walk up in the county like you the man of the joint. You knew how the county went and you fit right in crazy as that sounds. You knew the process and you knew it would be fast. In and out like a bank robbery. By the time you know it the time would have been slept off.

You go in and do your 4 days and on the fourth day in the morning they call your name to leave. You thought in your right mind that it was not that far of a walk to your house from the jail. Bullshit. You was an hour into your walk and you was not even halfway through the walk.

You decided to stop at the nearest bus stop and used your head and waited for the bus. Smartest thing you did since. The bus come and you jump on it like someone gave you some water in the middle of the desert with no water. Thank god. The bus drive was like 10 minutes. Funny.

You got off and enjoyed the walk only to walk into problems with the kids. You think that 4 days of county time for drinking would stop you but it did not. You was drinking that same night. In your head they were not going to test you just coming out of the county. The first day at the program they took your urine. Mother fucker. Done again.

You had another week out on the streets and you were back in the joint again but this time you had to do 5 days.

Chapter 10

Back in the jail with the correctional officers looking at you like you are another one of those inmates that will keep coming in and out of their jail. Not at all. In your head they wasn't going to see you as much because you don't plan on getting caught again.

You made friends in the jail and the ones that are still in there look at you like damn you coming back in the jail when they are trying to get out. It is always good to see them because they have questions on what the streets look like since they have been away.

While you are in jail you would be on the phone with your girlfriend asking about the pregnancy. She would give you a answer every time you would ask her. It almost felt like she knew what you was going to ask her. Premeditated answer. You paid attention to it but not really. You was just happy to be on the phone.

Once again your name is called and you pack up your stuff and you head out the door again. This time your girlfriend was there to get you with her friend, the neighbors girlfriend.

The ride was okay and you was silent most of the short ride. They both knew you were back home and whatever is out of place will be back in place. Fast! You get to the house and everyone knew you were home once you step foot out of the car. The neighbors girlfriend you called your drinking partner. That was funny. She drank shots all day long. You only drank at night.

This time you slowed down with the drinking. The program now knew that every time you took a urine send it out. They would call your name out of the blue. You were taking urines 3 to 4 times a week. After awhile they started giving you random 80 hour mouth swabs tests.

They had your number at the same time your girlfriend started slipping. She sent you a ultrasound picture of what she was having. She was having twins. You were amazed at the same time you were wondering what was taking so long to have the babies. You trusted her and would not think that she would lie to you about something like a pregnancy. So you thought.

You was so happy about the ultrasound picture you would show everybody. She would plan the doctors appointment on the days that you would go to the program. She knew that you could not miss any of the days unless it was an actual doctors appointment for yourself.

You were one day speaking to your counselor about what needs to be done as far as prevention. Not drinking. You never had a problem with drinking. They just think this is the best way to approach you being as though you are not addicted to any hard drugs. You got a phone call from your mother and she start by saying she was going to send you something and she did not want you to tell your girlfriend. You agreed and just listened even though you were in a meeting.

At the end of the phone call you looked at your phone because she sent you a text. The text was a picture of a website and a circle around a particular picture. It was the same exact picture your girlfriend sent you.

You showed your counselor and she stopped what she was talking about to bring up the website so she can see for herself. Damn if it was true. Your girlfriend took the photo off of internet and downloaded it to her phone then sent it to you and said the doctor sent it to her.

You counselor felt sorry for you. She didn't know what to say. She just told you to let it sink in and don't go home ready to hurt your soon to be ex girlfriend. You just went back to group and didn't say anything to the rest of the group.

You waited on the long ride home thinking about what you were going to say to her. What types of questions and responds you were going to get. You thought of everything and how you was going to not make it look like someone told you about the photo.

You got home and did not say anything right away. You act like you were tired and just wanted to relax. She was cooking some food and smoking a cigarette that she choses not to stop. Cool. In your head she may not be pregnant at all but still confused on how she looks pregnant.

You opened up the conversation with the normal. How is your day; What are you cooking; Where is the beer at? You was going to drink tonight for sure. You then asked her once she felt comfortable you asked her the question of looking at the email the doctors who did her ultrasound picture sent her.

The look on her face was priceless. She was shocked that you asked that question. She was not expecting that question. She grabbed her phone and was acting like she was going through her email to find it. You didn't pressure her because it was just funny to see her try knowing she didn't have it. The lies kept piling on and now it caught up with her.

She asked you why you wanted to see it. Your responds was to just see why the names was not on the pictures. She said she will find out when she go see them next week.

You then asked her why didn't they give her the paper photo. She said to you that they do it like that now. You rolled with it because she now know she is busted and it was just a matter of time before the whole thing blows up in her face and she wouldn't know how to explain it.

The night went different. You slept next to her but did not touch her and she noticed it. You needed a females in put on how she managed to look pregnant. I mean belly, eating habits, gain of weight, and all the things that came with a female and pregnancy. You went to slept with that on your mine knowing where to get the information from. The IOP program.

You wake up just in time for the van to come pick you up to take you to the program. You did not say goodbye to your soon to be ex girlfriend. All you told her was that you hope she had the email by the time you got back home. She had 3 hours to come up with another lie to keep it going but notice she can't.

107

She would have to come up with an email that has the same date that the email originally got sent to her. She was smart in this matter because she damn sure had you fooled for months but not that smart thinking you will over look it.

You get to the program and before everyone starts, they want to know what's going on with your situation. You sent the picture around then pulled up the exact same picture that was on the website and sent that around. They was shocked as you were because they were all believers as well.

The question now is how in the hell she looks pregnant? One of your older friends at the program spoke up and everyone listened . She told everyone that it could be a case of having an ovarian tumur or an ovarian siss. She further explained what causes it and what it does to a woman body. If not taken care of it could grow so big that it can make a female looks like she is pregnant. She can gain a eating habit and gain weight as if she was pregnant. The only difference was there is no baby.

That was the talk for awhile during the morning. You needed help coping with how you are going to deal with the fact that she has been telling you this lie for months and had your family believe she was as well but it was your family that was the ones that caught it first.

You go home ready to blow up in her face. The counselor had to help you come up with a way to deal with this matter the best way she knew how but understood as well. The answer you came up with was to go to your mothers house and live their and start over.

You are now home and you ask for answers and she had none. She was coming up with a story that you was trying to cause trouble in the house. You wanted to argue about things. You were frustrated that she still keeping this lie going . Its just a matter of time she going to actually have a baby or babies. Your mother said she is going to come up with one or two things. One she will say she lost one of the kids or she will say she lost them both. A mother is always right.

As you talked to your mother she was helping you deal with it on a day to day situation and a plan to leave, when, and how. You just could not deal with your soon to be ex girlfriend anymore. The day was coming where you got an eviction court date in the mail. You acted like you care but you seen it was a way out with ease.

Court day came and the landlord was at the courthouse. You guys had some things on him and he knew that if the judge sees it she was going to deny the eviction so he met you guys in the middle. You guys come up with the money owed to him within 2 weeks and the eviction was off but if not you definitely going to get evicted. Agreed

Two weeks has past and no money got produced. In this whole time the neighbor was telling the landlord all what you guys were doing nothing to come up with the money. The neighbor didn't really want you guys around for several reasons. He also wanted the house for his family. His girlfriend wanted to move next to your girlfriend because that was her friend and she wanted to get away from her boyfriend. That did not work and now you guys are his new target.

Two weeks past and the eviction was already in motion. He just gave you guys the benefit of a doubt because you guys were paying at one point and things do happen. Plus everyone loved money. You guys had one week to leave and the sheriff will come and kick your family out and padlock the door. That means you have a week to get your plan in order.

Within this week you had to talk to your probation officer and set a date to get your address changed. While this week was going on you was telling your counselor what your move was and to arrange a new way for a transportation that the program providing to get back and forth to the program from your mothers house. All is well and now you just have to play it by ear at home because you did not want your girlfriend to know your moves.

The neighbor was going to help you guys move the furniture to storage your girlfriend getting for the bigger things and the littler things that you guys may use in the day to day activities. She found a room at the motel down the street with 2 beds which still was not enough room. You had not only you and your girlfriend but she had both of her sons and one of their girlfriends. Let's remind you that you guys have 2 dogs and the motel they can't have dogs stay their over 20 pounds.

The day came to move out and the landlord along with the sheriff was there on time to padlock the doors. You and her sons had to put everything on the porch so everyone can see. The neighbor helped take all the big stuff to storage. While he was helping take your stuff to the motel, you were calling your mother to come get you. All you had was a suitcase, a duffle bag, a 42 inch tv, and one of the dogs. A blue pitbull that was only 1 years old and he loved you so you took him.

Once your mother showed up you put your things in the trunk and the dog with his cage in the back seat. You talked to your soon to be ex girlfriend about the move you were going to make and it made sense. She just wanted all of the family to go to your moms house. Her kids are very disrespectful and they were not allowed at your mothers to stay. Plus you were leaving her.

You gave her a little kiss then jumped in the car to go to your new home. Along the ride you was speaking about your move and how you will keep the program going from her house and how you were going to stay out of trouble. You would look out of the window and ask yourself, is this what your fate was????

Printed in the United States
By Bookmasters